The Book of Bill

Boris Black

Laurel
Highlands
Publishing

Laurel Highlands Publishing
Mount Pleasant, PA
USA

LaurelHighlandsPublishing.com

ISBN-13: 978-1-941087-21-3
ISBN-10: 1941087213

Acknowledgements:

I'd like to thank my editor, Veronica Moore, who dragged me, kicking and screaming, to a place where *The Book of Bill* became a far more engaging story.

For Helen and Carol

Do not distress yourself with dark imaginings.

And whether or not it is clear to you, no doubt the universe is unfolding as it should.

—Max Ehrmann

Part I

Jenna

In the Black Moshannon Forest, a fell beast roams, searching for warm flesh to rend and consume.

The creature runs freely through ninety thousand acres of state forestland. Bisecting the woods as if by a knife stroke is a scenic gorge, carved by the fury of the Little Kittanning River. In the western section, splashes of paint on boles of trees guide hikers and cross country skiers through well-maintained trails, and the smell of those who walk on two legs is always present. This is not to the beast's liking, and so, she locates a span of flat-water and swims across to the more desolate, eastern region of the forest.

In the eastern section, grey Poplar trunks and green, towering Firs cluster together like sentinels forbidding passage. Few humans ever come here, and odd, dark corners of the wood cling to secrets that pre-date mankind's industrial age. Sometimes, people get lost on the east side, or Calumet side, as the locals call it; and more than one adventurous hunter has lost his way, only to have his bones discovered years later.

The grey wolf, who thinks of herself as "Tyka," haunts the Calumet side of the Little Kittanning gorge. She has come from the north, traversing wilderness and macadam, living off small game, road kill, and the occasional garbage leavings. As it moved south, lonely two a.m. truckers fueled with amphetamines and Red Bull blinked and shook their heads at the grey form trotting along dark road shoulders. On and on, fording small streams and swimming larger rivers, Tyka finally arrived at her destination in the early Fall of the year. Now, she waits, not knowing why she has come or what her purpose might be.

One morning, not many weeks after arriving in the forest,

Tyka stops and sniffs the air. Something is coming. A great roar like a strengthening gale fills her mind. A profound silence follows the gale, and knowledge fills the void. The wolf's existence and purpose adopt new dimensions: She is a sentient, thinking being. It's like waking from a dream, and Tyka knows that the word "dream" is the correct human word for the visions that disturb her sleep.

For the first time, Tyka is a fully conscious entity; she is self-aware, knows that she is "wolf," and has been shaped into a unique life form. Her new-found consciousness does not burden Tyka with thoughts of morality.

As the season advances, dead leaves carpet the forest like a shroud. A sense of urgency grows in Tyka.

She has been called.

1:1

ill Miller knows about weakness. Not the physical kind—he benches three-twenty at the campus gym—but the inner kind. Bill tells himself lies that assume the semblance of truth. This shapes him into something he is not meant to be, and he ignores the small, quiet voice deep inside that defines his true character. He has not plumbed the depths of his discontent, nor does he know that it's as serious as it gets—for Bill questions his purpose, and wonders if he even has one.

An internal compass serves as a counterweight to Bill's weakness. His "true north" is a family man, responsible, respected, and respecting. He has a faithful wife, two beautiful, healthy children, and a fulfilling career. An assistant professor of sociology genuinely concerned about the intellectual development of his students, Bill labors, in his own small way, to advance human knowledge. As a father, he is patient and kind. As a husband, he is passionate, attentive, and faithful.

The pages of his life begin to turn more quickly when Bill

turns thirty-two. He comes to feel something is missing—a vital cog removed and mislaid that prevents him from operating as he should. Intellectual discussions with his wife, once a common occurrence, no longer appeal to him. When his daughter proudly displays a crayon drawing of a smiling family of four in front of a familiar-looking home, Bill is saddened when he struggles to give her the attention she has earned. Sometimes he wakes up in the middle of the night and stares for hours at swirls of plaster on the ceiling. He thinks about the passing years and how quickly the kids are growing. Troubling questions nag at him: *Is this all there is? Is there nothing more? Why can't I be happy?*

Bill intuits that if he lives until he's eighty, he'll look back and feel like his life passed in the blink of an eye. *You marry a good woman. You love her as well as you can. You bring children into the world, and raise them with kindness. Along the way, you make a contribution in your field; perhaps infect a few students with a passion for knowledge and learning. Then you grow old. If you're lucky, you don't forget who the hell you are toward the end. Then you shit your pants, and maybe die screaming in pain from penile cancer.*

"Life's a bitch, then, you die," Bill observes. He complains to his friend, Steve Lendowski, as they sit in the booth of a pub not far from the Glenville University campus. Steve's a fifty-five year old English professor with a salt-and-pepper beard, a bright twinkle in large brown eyes, and a hippy outlook on life that provides an appropriate counterpoint to Bill's brooding demeanor. Steve also has a low tolerance for bullshit, and will not let Bill get away with shoveling it.

"Yeah, man, you've got it rough," Steve says, rolling his eyes. "Beautiful wife other men would kill to be with. Two great kids.

Nice career with good pay. Hell, I feel bad for you, man. If I were you, I'd probably just curl into a ball and give up."

"Fuck you, Steve." Bill is not angry—only a little drunk. He takes another pull on his *Rolling Rock,* saying, "It's just... we're all just dust, waiting to blow away. You know? I mean, what's the point? You make love to your wife. You teach a class. And in a hundred years, no one will even remember I lived."

Steve drains the last of his beer, shrugs, and leans forward with his elbows on the table—serious now. "Look, Bill, it's like this. Two kinds of people in the world, right? One guy says life is meaningless; the other one thinks there's a purpose—maybe something better waiting for him on the other side. I can't tell you which guy is right. But, I know the type I am. Which is why I'm going to get laid—can't let my rep as Glenville's most horny bachelor lapse. Happy trails, buddy."

Steve gives Bill a wink and a slap on the shoulder. He slides out of the booth and saunters over to a very nice-looking redhead at the bar. Within a few seconds, she's laughing at something Steve has said, and Bill thinks maybe his friend has a pretty reasonable philosophy about the meaning of life. He leaves Steve to his imminent conquest—another in a long series.

Driving home from the bar with a moderate buzz, Bill thinks about what Steve said. *What type am I? If life has no higher purpose, that's a pretty good argument for going after what you want—and to hell with the consequences.*

He drives past contemporary suburban houses with large front lawns to a quiet cul-de-sac. Bill parks in his driveway and sits in the car for five minutes, thinking. It's late, past ten-o-clock. The house, a contemporary cape cod, is dark except for a flicker of grey light from the television flashing through a crack in the curtains.

Is this all there is? Is there nothing more? What type am I?

Bill thinks about his family. He thinks about Stacey. Bill has shown his wife his true north, and has no doubt she loves him for it. But, he's also allowed her to become well-acquainted with his weaknesses. Sometimes the compass goes awry, magnetic forces (or the male libido) send the inner needle spinning in all directions. Bills understands that Stacey, a paralegal and reader of non-fiction, is not naïve—knows there's nothing like a twenty-year old co-ed in tight jeans to get his compass needle spinning.

A ruffle of curtains at the living room window captures Bill's attention. Stacey peeks through the gap in the drapes and stares at Bill just sitting there in the car. The curtains fall back in place. A moment later, the exterior light comes on above the front door. Bill gets out of the car and slowly shuffles up the walk. He opens the door and goes inside.

The television is still on, but the entire downstairs is empty. *She must have run up the steps, no doubt pissed I came home late.* Bill turns off the TV. The house is eerily quiet. The enormous tick of the grandfather clock in the foyer is forbidding.

For some minutes, Bill stands alone in the living room. He feels lost—like he never really came home.

Is this all there is? Why can't I be happy? What type am I?

On the first day of the fall semester, Bill strolls confidently into his ten a.m. Introduction to Sociology class, stumbles, and drops his lecture notes in a shower of fluttering papers. A young blonde sits front-row center. Her smile suggests she knows all Bill's secrets. She wears cut-off denim shorts, a tight, white t-shirt that caresses erect nipples, and scarlet high heels—a goddess dressed like a slut.

Bill's face reddens. When he squats to pick up his notes, he can't stop himself from glancing up at the girl's cream-colored legs, waxed and lightly tanned, crossed a few feet in front of his nose. A few chuckles spatter the classroom. Nearly frantic, Bill hurriedly gathers the pages together in a loose pile, feeling as if he's in the midst of some slow-motion, erotic nightmare. When he stands and dares to look her in the face, she smiles and rests the thick end of a pen on full, crimson lips, slightly parted. Then she slowly slides the pen into her mouth, and Bill forgets for a moment that there are twenty other students in the room.

Somehow, Bill manages to get through that first class. He does his best to maintain a professional attitude, but his eyes are constantly drawn back to his desire. The girl torments Bill by arching her back and crossing and uncrossing silky legs. She smiles in such a way that Bill knows he can have her.

Over the next week, Bill thinks of little else. Jenna is a stunning standout in class, responding to questions regarding arcane sociological theory with lucidity—and has a lascivious smile. She is tall, very tall, five-eleven, with the angelic face of a teen tempered by some ineffable quality in the liquid pale blue eyes that is normally and justifiably reserved for sophisticated middle-aged women approaching their sexual prime.

The temptation is that much worse because it's obvious to Bill, based on the sultry looks he gets from Jenna, that the attraction is mutual. Bill is not conceited, but neither is he surprised that Jenna finds him attractive. He has a thirty-four inch waist, broad shoulders, a square chin, piercing grey eyes, and a distinguished fleck of early white in his black wavy hair. A brooding, saturnine mien adds to the overall effect. During his five years of teaching, there had been numerous unmistakable signals from the young ladies and a few outright offers of sex. But, Bill had never seriously considered cheating on Stacey—until Jenna.

Bill dreams of her full lips, shoulder length blonde hair, and flawless skin, nearly translucent in its perfection. A beauty mark low down on her left cheek is the finishing touch on a face and figure that might have been sculpted by some artistic perfectionist. And, there is that indefinable, subtle quality—maturity beyond her years, perhaps—which draws Bill to her.

In class, Jenna does not disguise the fact that she is fully aware of Bill's desire. She frequently bends forward at her desk. Bill gives in, staring as full, cream-colored breasts come tantalizingly close to bursting out of low-cut sweaters. He loses his place during lectures more than once. Observing Bill's discomfiture, Jenna adopts a faux pout, playfully taunting Bill because she's managed to distract him yet again. Other students in the class don't miss the build-up of sexual tension. The boys mostly smirk, and the girls look pissed. Bill doesn't care.

As the weeks pass, Bill's desire ripens into torment—he must have her! He frequently fantasizes about Jenna and masturbates in the shower. Sex with his wife has lost much of its appeal. Bill wants Jenna and no other. *I'll ask her to stay after class so we can arrange to meet at the Holiday Inn.*

The day following his resolution to make a move, Bill sits in his campus office and stares at a pile of student essays, thinking about Jenna. *The honeyed brush of her lips on his neck. Inside of her, gripped tight like a too-small glove. Ankles wrapped around the small of his back.* A soft knock at the open door causes him to look up. Wearing jeans so tight they might have been painted on, Jenna has a look in her eyes Bill has seen in women before. Her steady gaze conveys to Bill that Jenna has a deep, smoldering hunger.

"I need to talk to you," she says, and Bill becomes fully engorged so quickly he becomes dizzy.

"How can I help you?" Bill manages, trying to be cool.

"Well, I have this problem—I thought maybe you could help me, *Professor*." She nudges the office door closed with a little wiggle of her hip. Perky nipples push out the soft cotton of her pink tank top. Bill begins to rise, but she's already on her knees, crawling to him on all fours like a slinky feline. Bill collapses back into the chair.

"I need this," Jenna murmurs, lowering her head. Bill breathes deep the clean, shampoo smell of her hair. She unzips him. Bill groans when she wraps her hand around his shaft. Jenna slips him between her plump lips.

After she finishes him off, Jenna wipes semen from her lips with the back of her hand. She grins in a way Bill hasn't seen before. He thinks it's a look of self-satisfaction—a look of victory. Bill has a moment of doubt. *What's her game?* But his uncertainty passes quickly. He grins back at her, feeling pretty good about himself. *Hell, what red-blooded university professor hasn't fantasized about what just happened?*

When she shows up at Bill's office the next day, he jumps out of his chair and closes the door himself. Jenna kicks off her heels, then sits on the edge of his desk, lips lightly parted.

Bill says, "Let's get you out of those jeans," and she obligingly lifts her hips as he pulls them off.

She lies back on the desk—legs bent at the knee and spread wide. Delirious, Bill plants light kisses on her smooth inner thighs, then slides off her panties with his teeth. She has shaved herself, further exciting him. He works north until his face and tongue are where they want to stay forever.

Jenna begins to moan. She thrusts her hips forward, grinding into Bill's face. Her entire body quivers, then her thighs slap the sides of Bill's head in an involuntary spasm as she climaxes.

Jenna rolls over on her stomach. She slides down the desk, putting her feet on the floor. Bill drops his pants quickly, desperate to get inside of her. He enters her from behind. He rocks her slowly at first, working hard not to come. Jenna emits a low, primal moan. Bill can't hold back any longer. He thrusts violently, penetrating her as deep as he can go. Bill's entire body goes rigid. Jenna cries out at the same time Bill explodes inside of her.

When he pulls out, Jenna turns around and puts him in her mouth. The pleasure becomes extreme, a torment. For a time, the entity that is Bill ceases to exist—there is only mindless pleasure.

For a couple of days after the office sex, Bill struts around the campus. He only begins to think about how he may have placed his career in jeopardy when the frumpy administrative assistant gives him an odd look. *Does she know?* He nods to colleagues in the faculty lounge, who whisper behind their hands. *Relax, they*

can't prove anything. Rick Harmon passes Bill in the hall and says, "How's your *wife*, Bill?" *Shit—just how thin are the walls between our offices?*

Bill decides he'd better move "play-time" off campus. Jenna is the best piece of tail he's ever had, but it's not worth his job. Still thinking mostly with his penis, Bill doesn't even consider the possibility that he could also ruin his marriage.

He stresses the need for discretion with Jenna, but the admonition is completely unnecessary. She is totally cool—no melodrama, no head games, just a good time. They have sex in his car, out in the woods, under a fir tree, and in an inexpensive motel. As the weeks pass, Bill's fondness for Jenna grows. He knows he's getting carried away, but the idea that his affair is a temporary thing becomes unthinkable.

One evening after a few beers in their favorite booth, Bill confides in Steve.

"And, it's not just the great sex," Bill says. "She listens attentively and provides cogent remarks about departmental politics, and critiqued my paper on pathologies in the homeless like a professional academic. She pegged Stacey as a control freak right off. I know it's a cliché, but the truth is, Steve, she *does* understand me."

Steve just about chokes on his beer. "Right, man, and I'm sure that tight little ass has nothing to do with it."

Bill laughs. "Damn, Steve, why'd you go and do that? I was just beginning to believe my own bullshit." Bill grins and clinks Steve's mug of beer with his own.

"Just be careful," Steve says. "You have plenty to lose, my friend."

Bill grins again, feeling too good to consider unpleasant possibilities.

He sees Jenna as often as he can. The Holiday Inn out by the airport becomes their favorite spot. One time, lying next to her after another round of mind-blowing sex, Bill gives the perfectly contoured ass cheek a little pinch. He says, "Sweetie, just how is it you've managed to become a world-champion sex artist at such a tender age?"

Jenna curls up to him, tweaking his left nipple between sharp fingernails.

"Ouch, you little bitch!" Bill says, giving her a playful slap on the ass.

Adopting a naughty-little-girl's voice, Jenna says, "You're my first, Daddy." Then surprises Bill by speaking in German, Japanese, and Latin. After demanding a translation, Bill finds that her statements are suitably smutty.

Damn, Bill thinks. *A virtuoso at fellatio AND multi-lingual. This girl's a freak. Not that I'm complaining.* Too infatuated with Jenna to consider for long the unusual nature of her worldly sophistication, Bill just accepts it as another lucky break.

Bill lies to his wife about evening seminars, committee meetings, late office hours, and campus recruitment events. He'd slept with Stacey a couple of times after he started with Jenna, but then nothing for the last six weeks. He makes excuses about being tired or stressed out. Stacey doesn't say anything, let alone make a move of her own. Bill figures she must be getting suspicious. *You*

don't sleep with someone at least a couple of times a week for eight straight years, then go cold turkey and not wonder what's up. Then again, fuck it—she can't prove anything as long as I'm careful.

Bill revels in his infidelity. The barrier that separates him from Stacey becomes a wall of granite. Communication in the marriage devolves into Stacey snapping at Bill for no particular reason. Bill responds as nicely as he can, maintaining the pretense that nothing is wrong. He even gives her little pecks on the cheek from time to time. *She will not bait me. She will not undermine my happiness.* When Stacey suggests that Bill start sleeping on the futon in the den, he pretends to be hurt.

One morning while eating a bowl of cold cereal in the breakfast nook, Bill realizes Stacey hasn't spoken a word to him for two days. She's scrubbing dishes with her back turned to him. Just to break the silence, he asks, "Hey, Stace, what should we get the kids for Christmas?" She doesn't answer. Bill shrugs and goes back to his cereal.

A few minutes later as she walks out of the kitchen, Stacey shoots Bill a look he hasn't seen before. She doesn't say a word, just pads up the stairs to the bedroom. It takes Bill a moment to interpret her glance. *I disgust her.* The thought is a shock, and the epiphany about what Stacey thinks of him finally breaks through the wall Bill had erected.

She must know. But how? And how could I have had my head so far up my own ass?

Over the next few days, Bill's true character begins to reemerge and clamor for attention. Thoughts of the pain he must be inflicting on Stacey nag at him. An internal battle rages. He finally remembers that he still loves his wife. But he doesn't want to lose Jenna, either.

Bill imagines those silly cartoons where a guy has a little angel on one shoulder telling him to do the right thing, and on the other shoulder is a little devil whispering that he should do what he wants. *"You need to give up Jenna,"* says the little angel, and then the little devil whispers in the opposite ear, *"No!—just a few more weeks! You can have it all!"*

The compass needle spins.

Not long before Thanksgiving, Bill and Jenna are back in the Holiday Inn. After sex, Jenna curls up on his chest like a purring kitten. She runs her fingers lightly over the curly, black hair on his chest, then slides her hand down to gently squeeze the head of his penis. Bill is capable of going again, but for the first time in the relationship, he rolls away from Jenna instead of giving her what she wants. A sudden thought occurs to Bill seemingly from no-where.

The spirit is willing; the flesh is weak.

He blurts, "You know, I wouldn't have had to cheat if Stacey had initiated sex every once in a while."

Jenna sits up with a white sheet around her body. She looks surprised at the sudden, unexpected comment. Then she grins—a mischievous glint in her eyes. "Ahhh, does Mommy powder baby's bottom before the diaper goes on?" Then, apparently without malice, but with sympathy and understanding, "C'mon, Bill, you don't need to have your ego massaged by Stacey initiating sex. At least be honest with yourself. This is about you being married for a long time, and you just wanted something different."

Bill knows the ugly truth when he hears it—has done his best to suppress it for several months. They get dressed in silence after that.

He drives Jenna back toward her dorm. She fiddles with the radio, going from country to rock to some asshole spouting hellfire and damnation. After several minutes, Bill says, "I don't want to give you up, Jen, but Stacey can never know. She doesn't deserve the hurt—my betrayal."

Jenna pouts—or pretends to. She slouches down in the passenger seat. She puts her feet up on the dash, bare legs bent at the knees as if she's ready to give birth. Working on the knob of a lollypop like she can make it come, she tells Bill what he wants to hear: "It's okay, baby, most men aren't satisfied with meat and potatoes every night of the week. It's only natural."

Bill embraces the "everybody-does-it" rationalization. He knows the bad excuse for what it is; but eyeing Jenna, he becomes aroused. Bill says, feeling oh-so-clever, "Forget the potatoes, I've got your meat right here."

Then he finds a place to pull the car over so they can go again.

⚔ 1:2 ⚔

F *ucking bastard.*

He's probably screwing some nineteen year old twit from one of his classes. Stacey is deeply suspicious of Bill. She doesn't know for sure, but the likelihood of his infidelity grows with each passing day.

Stacey rams Bill's dirty laundry into the washing machine. Jeff, their black lab, flinches when she slams the lid. The dog gives Stacey a doleful look.

"Don't give me those big eyes," Stacey says, scratching Jeff under the chin. She opens the French doors in the laundry room that lead to the back yard. Jeff bounds out and lifts his leg on a mimosa. "You're not the only dog in the house, are you, boy?" Stacey wants to laugh at her poor joke, but can't manage it.

Bill has been spending more and more evenings at the campus—or so he claims. The job had never required it before. Stacey finds his excuses to be tiresome and disrespectful. He doesn't answer his cell, and rarely even bothers to text to let her know he can't talk. *And after eight years of marriage, he's suddenly too stressed-out to make love? Bullshit.*

Stacey pads out to the kitchen and pours herself a cup of coffee. The house is pleasingly quiet. Bill teaches Tuesday mornings, Krista is at morning kindergarten, and the baby is down for his nap. She sits in the breakfast nook, savoring the strong, black coffee. It's a good time to think.

After the second cup, Stacey gets up from the kitchen table and paces the linoleum. By the time the washer has gone through its cycle, Stacey figures she's lucky she hasn't worn a groove in the kitchen tile. *Am I losing my husband? Does he still love me? Am I even sure he's cheating?* The idea of Bill's likely betrayal makes Stacey feel like a failure as a wife—as if she is deficient for having neglected to keep her husband content.

I'll wait. If he's doing what I think he's doing, he'll slip up sooner or later. Then we'll see.

No trust. No marriage.

Weeks pass. Stacey becomes numb. She tries to summon anger, sadness, and tears—all those reactions she knows she should experience, but can't. She even pinches her forearm to feel physical pain—to prove to herself that she *can* feel. When Billy throws a container of yogurt on the kitchen floor, Stacey doesn't react as the toddler shrieks his protest; she just stares vacantly at the puddle of food on the tile. Finally snapping out of it, she thinks, *It's like somebody's drugged me with a powerful tranquilizer. Must be some kind of a defense mechanism.*

"Order out for pizza tonight," "Krista needs to be picked up at daycare on Thursday," "Jeff has fleas," and "I'll be at the office until eight" are the only things Stacey says to Bill for days at a time. She imagines that she's a lifeless automaton, going through simulated motions. Unable to focus on work, she takes a leave of absence from her part-time job as a paralegal in the Rose and Greenwood law firm.

Bill continues to come home late and acts like everything in the marriage is fine. The sudden absence of intimacy after being close to Bill for so long is a shock. Stacey misses the feel of his arms around her, the caress of his hand on her cheek, and the clean smell of him after a morning shower. Too proud to initiate, she becomes even more frustrated as Bill keeps to his side of the bed night after night. She considers confronting him, but fears the outcome. *What if he lies straight to my face? What if he doesn't even bother to deny it?* The idea of confirming Bill's betrayal produces a hollowness in her stomach, like something vital has been removed by a careless surgeon.

Stacey confides in her friend, Amy, while trying to scald her throat on a latte. They're seated in the Starbucks café, a sprinkle of customers chattering about them. "It's maddening," Stacey says to her friend. "I snap at him just to get a reaction, and the son-of-a-bitch gives me a kiss on the cheek like that'll fix everything."

"Well, I'm not going to blow smoke up your ass and tell you not to worry," Amy says. "It doesn't sound good." Stacey and Amy became good friends while she helped Amy with her cases at the Rose and Greenwood firm. She has a reputation for making assistant district attorneys and any lawyer sitting on the opposite bench cower in courthouse bathrooms. Stacey doesn't know how she managed alone—a widow at a young age who raised three kids. The auburn beauty did it all while advancing to junior partner.

"It's just... I don't know," Stacey says, throwing up her hands and letting them fall to the tabletop with a clunk. "The situation is absurd. All this pretending."

"Agreed," Amy replies. "Which is why you can't continue to drive yourself crazy. You either confront him or get one of our investigators to follow him around."

A private investigator. Is this really happening to me? Stacey glances around at the folks seated at little square tables. Amy takes a pull on her Frappuccino, eyeing Stacey over the brim of the cup. A good-looking guy—slim waist, dark hair, broad shoulders, can't yet be thirty—makes eye contact with Stacey and smiles. She quickly looks away.

Amy catches the exchange. Smiling, she says, "There you go, sweetie, you could go have a good, hard grudge fuck."

Stacey laughs with a hint of bitterness. Playing along, she says, "No, too much trouble. I'd have to wipe his nose and tell him how good he is in bed. Stroke his ego. Maybe you could just loan me Dr. Phil, Amy."

It's Amy's turn to laugh. Dr. Phil is the name she's given her vibrator.

They change the subject and chat some about the office. Stacey can feel the younger guy still checking her out, but she doesn't give him any hope. Out in the lot when they part, Amy says, "Don't forget what I told you, Stacey. You have to make a move. You owe it to yourself."

When the leaves change from gold to brown and start falling from the trees, Stacey still has not confronted Bill—nor has she resorted to hiring a detective. The paralysis she feels extends to minor, daily decisions she must make. One evening, the conundrum of whether to prepare chicken or fish for dinner becomes a source of indecision and anxiety. *Jesus. I'm a fucking mess.*

The distance between the couple is a chasm filled with jagged rocks. Bill continues merrily on his way, coming up with a different excuse nearly every night of the week. He doesn't even seem to miss seeing Krista and Billy, who are tucked in and sleeping hours before he finally makes an appearance. For Stacey, the situation has become intolerable. The numbness slowly erodes. Her anger bubbles like lava just beneath the surface, threatening to erupt.

No trust. No marriage.

When he comes home one night after eleven, Stacey suggests that Bill sleep on the futon in the den. He manages to look hurt and puzzled, but doesn't even put up a fight. *Son-of-a-bitch might as well hang a big guilty sign around his neck.*

Alone in their king-sized bed that night, Stacey cries for the first time over the apparent demise of her marriage. Great, silent sobs wrack her body as she hugs her knees to her chest.

She finally drifts off to sleep sometime after midnight—and dreams of Bill. They are seated together on a blanket next to a still lake that shines like a mirror. He puts his arm around her, and she puts her head on his shoulder. It is a moment of perfect contentment, which is soon spoiled by the sound of a woman moaning.

Stacey turns her head away from Bill to find the source of the sounds. Female moans and masculine grunts of pleasure surge to an apex. Stacey opens her eyes. She is wide awake; there is no fuzziness between the dream and waking reality. Downstairs in the den, the unbridled racket of lovers arriving at sexual climax comes to a sudden halt. *He's fucking her in our home. In our home. With his children sleeping a couple yards away. In our HOME.*

Stacey is paralyzed. She wants to storm down the stairs and confront them, but she can't move. She imagines she is a statue. *No, I'm a corpse. No pain. No memories. I am nothing.*

Out in front of the house, a motorcycle splinters the silence of the quiet, suburban street. She didn't hear the girl leave the house—*bitch is quiet as a mouse when she isn't screwing my husband*—but is convinced the cycle with big pipes has carried off the slut who wrecked her marriage.

This isn't living. I am a corpse. I am nothing.

After a minute, Stacey's fingers begin to tingle from hyperventilation—the first return of feeling to her body. The numbness she has felt for weeks is gone. She clenches her hands into fists until it hurts.

Padding to the bathroom, Stacey flicks on the light. She's broken several, well-manicured nails on both hands. She washes blood from the wounds in her palms. Looking in the mirror over the sink, she is surprised at her expression.

Didn't know I could hate that much. Better than the numbness, though. No more robot. No more corpse. And, I think I'll just skip the whole heartbreak stage. Hold onto the anger for a while—at least until I take him down in court.

No trust. No marriage.

They met in graduate school. When he walked into the Law and Society seminar, Stacey turned to a girl beside her and said, "Holy shit." Bill looked like a model for Abercrombie and Fitch—only more rugged and handsome. It took him a month to ask her out, though he confessed on their initial date that he'd wanted to the minute he first saw her. A few drinks with dinner relaxed them both. Light-hearted disagreements about law and society trended to relationships, life, and what they wanted out of it. Bill managed a few goofy jokes. Stacey laughed, and they were on their way.

At first, the relationship was based on little more than torrid sex. Red flags reared up and waved about almost immediately. She thought he was too full of himself, perhaps self-indulgent. They had a terrible argument three weeks into the relationship over something trivial neither of them could remember later, split for two days, and came together again with the best make-up sex ever. They talked for a long time after that, and discovered that in addition to the mutual physical attraction, they genuinely liked each other.

In those early days of the relationship, they talked for hours without getting tired. When the conversation faltered, the silences felt natural and comfortable. Three months after the first date, they got an apartment together. In another three months, they had a plan. Fast forward six more months, and the pair were a happily married couple.

"Marry in haste, repent in leisure," Stacey's mother, Isabella, pronounced at the small reception—but neither Stacey nor Bill was bothered by it, because they just *knew* what they had together would last forever.

The marriage, like most, had some problems. "You need to work on that lazy streak, Bill," Stacey would say.

Then Bill would try to keep it light with rejoinders like "Don't try to change me, baby."

A persistent source of conflict involved Stacey's deferred career aspirations. Although they jointly decided to put Stacey's law education on hold while she worked and he finished his doctorate, she grew to resent this. But then, Bill successfully defended his dissertation, and a tenure stream offer came in from Glenville State University. Glenville was a nice place for Bill to start his career, and the region was upscale with good schools. The young couple developed a circle of friends in the community and enjoyed commingling at college functions. They started talking about having a baby.

When Bill accepted the assistant professorship at Glenville, Stacey thought she'd glimpsed the opening to go back and finish her own studies—the Duquesne Law School was only an hour away. But Bill wanted a child, and Stacey was not very resistant. Law school could wait. First little Krista, a dark beauty who favored Stacey, and then three years later a little black-haired bruiser named Billy took over their lives. (Isabella observed that it was a shame two educated people would have children so close together).

When diapers finally became a thing of the past, Stacey accepted a position as a paralegal to supplement Bill's average salary. The resentment lingered—Stacey knew she had the capacity to become an attorney in a significant firm. Bill was oblivious to all of this.

But, Bill didn't stick a gun to Stacey's head. She willingly stopped taking birth control pills, and the children—poop, tears, and all—were a joy. Krista and Billy bound the couple, and through the financial strain and personality clashes, their relationship matured, and over time became stable in a way that transcended those attachments based solely on passionate, physical love.

Stacey's love for Bill became inseparable from her identity. It was a love that acknowledged and encompassed all of his flaws. She would die for Bill—and kill for him, if necessary.

Stacey vividly remembers a night not long after Billy was born when Bill asked her why she loved him. It was one in the morning, and the baby had finally gone to sleep. They were just holding each other, too exhausted for lovemaking. It was a good moment, and Stacey felt like they were in a place where growing old together was a comfortable certainty.

She'd thought about Bill's question for a few seconds, then couldn't resist having some fun. She replied, "Why, darling, because of your massive dick, of course." Bill laughed at that, and hugged her tighter.

She said, "You make me feel special, Bill. I love you because of how you hyperventilated when I went into labor with Krista. Do you remember that old nurse who wanted to kick you out of the delivery room, and asked if you were going to be okay? You blurted, 'I'm just worried about Stacey!' I love you because you never clear the snow off your car without doing mine first. You dote over me like a mother hen every time I get a sniffle. Because of your loud, ridiculous laugh when you watch cartoons with

Krista. The way you look at me. I love you because when you hold me, I feel safe, like nothing can ever hurt me. I know I love you, husband, because I still would, even if you didn't love me back."

Stacey did not feel the need to ask the same question of Bill, knowing in her heart he felt the same way. It was a perfect moment.

Stacey's last words to Bill that night were not put to the test for two years.

After that night when he had his mistress in the den, Stacey internalizes her anger and ignores Bill completely. She doesn't speak to him or make eye contact for days.

The week of Thanksgiving arrives. The Glenville campus closes for the holiday. Stacey is surprised when Bill spends his time around the house and doesn't even go out in the evenings. *What happened? Did the little slut dump him?* Curious, Stacey maintains her glacial distance, and even takes some pleasure when she observes that her "cold shoulder" causes Bill some discomfiture. *Oh, this is good. Next, he'll act innocent, and ask 'What's wrong, baby?'*

Stacey makes it through the holiday, including a painful dinner where her mother rolls her eyes and breaks the silence with frequent throat clearings. Stacey will not confide in Isabella. *She's too judgmental. All I'd hear is what I did wrong. When I set things in motion—then she can know.*

The Monday after Thanksgiving, Stacey answers the phone in the kitchen and receives an unexpected and disturbing message. A man's voice says, "Stacey," then proceeds to impart information about Bill's anatomy that only Stacey and the family physician ought to know.

"Who is this?" Stacey asks, gripping the phone with whitened knuckles.

"The name of the co-ed your husband was nailing is Jenna," the man says. "Just thought you'd like to know." He chuckles, and breaks the connection. Stacey stands there for a minute with the dial tone buzzing in her ear.

Bill, what kind of a freak show did you turn this marriage into? The knowledge that Bill's mistress had imparted intimate details about her husband to some unknown man—who takes delight in Stacey's humiliation—is the crowning insult. *The whole thing is obscene.*

She finally hangs up the phone and collapses at the breakfast nook. A sudden realization hits her like a rock to the face. *I will never forgive him.*

No trust. No marriage.

Stacey calls her mother and asks her to babysit. "Not now, Mom," she says on her way out the door in response to Isabella's demand for an explanation. Stacey hits the highway and heads east into the mountains. She drives for hours along little traveled rural routes, enjoying the solitude and the steady hum of the car.

By the time she pulls into the driveway that evening, Stacey has suppressed her anger in favor of rational, clinical thought. She thanks her mother, practically shoves her out the door, and puts the kids to bed early. Bill isn't home.

Stacey sheds her clothes and takes a long, pleasurable shower. Krista and Billy are sleeping deeply—no worries. After the shower, Stacey stands naked in front of the master bedroom's full length mirror. She looks hard at herself—no blinking—and justifiably concludes that her one-hundred and fifteen pound body is tight and well-formed. *A flat tummy, nice tits I didn't ruin with breastfeeding, and a petite, heart-shaped bottom—not bad.* She feels the streak of white hair that has emerged in her raven-black hair these past few months is especially attractive and compliments her smooth, Mediterranean complexion. Looking deep into her own dark eyes staring out of the mirror, Stacey concludes, *Now, there's a woman one ought NOT fuck with.*

She turns away from the mirror and pulls on her underwear, jeans, and a sweater. The truth of her marital situation settles in with absolute clarity. What had been love is compartmentalized and stowed away, like an artifact in a museum.

I don't need a psychologist or priest to tell me the problem with the marriage is not because of some deficiency on my part. Hell, Bill would have cheated if I looked like Liz Taylor. The penis is not a discriminating or faithful organ—not my fault!

"I don't even have to take his infidelity personally," she says, walking down the stairs and punching numbers on her cell phone.

Stacey feels good and very confident. *I've washed off Bill's bullshit. And I don't have to let anymore get on me.* She makes an appointment with the family law specialist at the Rose and Greenwood firm.

No trust. No marriage.

⊰ 1:3 ⊱

"Jenna, I need to see you in my office," Bill says after proctoring an exam before Thanksgiving break. She was the final student to turn in the test. They are alone in the classroom.

Jenna shoots Bill that sultry look that arouses him instantly. "Okay, Professor," she says. "I could use a good, *stiff* tutoring."

Damn, she looks more beautiful than ever. This is going to be tough. But, I've got to stick to my guns. Stacey is on to me, and I can't lose my family.

Jenna follows Bill down to his office. As soon as the door closes, she moves close to Bill and brushes her hand lightly over the front of his pants. He slaps her hand away.

"Okay, baby, let's play," she says and pushes him back against the chair behind his desk. Off balance, Bill falls into a sitting position. Jenna gets on her knees. She grabs Bill's engorged member through his khakis. He groans with pleasure when she takes it out and slides all of him in her mouth.

Remember what's important.

The voice comes from inside Bill's mind. *That was strange,* he thinks, distracted from Jenna's rapidly bobbing head. *Almost like someone whispered the words in my ear.* He'd been close to ejaculation, but now he's losing his erection. The words echo through Bill's cranium like an object set in motion by an immutable, Newtonian law.

Remember what's important... important... important.

Bill becomes half-limp inside of Jenna's mouth. She looks up at Bill. She stands and takes three staggering steps backwards. Eyebrows raised, jaw dropped in amazement, Jenna says, "You've got to be fucking kidding me."

Bill stands and makes himself decent. "It's over, Jenna. I love my wife."

"But not enough to resist fucking me for the last three months, huh?" Jenna does not conceal her anger. "Do you really love her, Bill? If you do, do you even know why?"

"Because I love her with my soul," Bill replies immediately. "I love her in my gut—would jump in front of a train if it would save her life. I saw the crowns of two little heads emerge from her body. She made this sound when the kids were born. It was a cry of joy. I love her because of how she brushes a strand of hair back from my forehead and the way she runs her hand lightly up and down my back when we're with company. She gets this hot look when she wants me. I love her because of the little birthmark on her left hip. Because when I hold her in the night it feels more *right* than anything I've ever known. When I hold her nothing else matters, not even the future. When we make love, it's like... like we're... one flesh."

Bill stops suddenly when he realizes how the words had tum-

31

bled out in a rush—almost as if they'd been placed in his mouth by some external force. *But, it's all true. I love Stacey, forever.*

Jenna glares at Bill with such malice that he takes an involuntary step backwards. All of her beauty seems to vanish in a blur of motion. It's just a micro-second, but for a moment, Bill thinks he can see Jenna as she truly is—on the inside. *Not so beautiful after all.*

The vision of the "ugly" Jenna is gone in a flicker of time. She smiles with faux sweetness and gives Bill the finger. "Go fuck yourself, asshole."

Jenna struts out of the office and does not look back.

That evening, Bill intuits a change in Stacey. She puts a plate of ziti in front of him and walks off. The cold distance has been replaced by a look of self-assurance. *What happened? Did she find out about Jenna? Am I going to lose my family?*

Stacey puts the kids to bed early and retires to their bedroom without so much as a "good night." Bill tosses about on the futon in the den. Giving up on sleep, he quietly climbs the stairs and looks in on Krista. The girl favors Stacey, and looks exceptionally beautiful as she sleeps. Bill kneels at her bedside. After five minutes, a single tear slips down his cheek. Across the hall, his son sleeps in his little racecar bed. One chubby leg has slipped over the side. Bill gently places the toddler's leg back under the blanket and caresses a curl of hair off his forehead.

Remember what's important.

The voice, so very real, comes from inside Bill—from a still, quiet place where his weaknesses are crushed with walls of granite. The voice is an affirmation that, come what may, he has made a turn in the right direction.

When Bill finally drifts off to sleep, he experiences the most erotic dream of his life. It's Jenna. She's on top of him, grinding and thrusting so hard the pleasure becomes pain. She digs sharp nails into his chest. When he ejaculates, it's as if every ounce of fluid is draining from his body. After the orgasm, his skin feels like insects are crawling over it. The dream perspective shifts so that Bill is looking down on his own body as it lay on the futon. He is a mottled corpse. Maggots crawl hungrily across his face and wriggle inside of empty eye sockets.

Bill wakes, barely stifling a scream. He brushes frantically at his arms and face.

Jesus Christ. That was so fucking real. And, God help me, I liked it. At least, until the end.

Bill does not sleep the remainder of the night.

When classes resume after Thanksgiving, Bill is both disappointed and relieved that Jenna does not attend Intro to Sociology. Part of him still wants her—*yeah, the dick part*—but the relief is greater than the disappointment. Taking Steve's advice, Bill divulges the past relationship with Jenna to Peg Smith in human resources. *That should cover my ass—I hope.*

Conditions at home become unbearable. Stacey will not respond to Bill's attempts at communication. *Does she know for sure? What's her plan? Did I really think ending things with Jenna would magically restore my marriage?* He marvels at his stupidity, a supposed intellectual who'd been unable to see beyond his next erection. Asking him to sleep on the futon had been a wake-up call even his lust for Jenna could not cloud. However, Stacey's silence since he'd come to his senses and ended the fling is far more disconcerting.

Bill gives up trying to talk to her, and studies every move on her face. What he sees there scares him more than the erotic nightmares that continue to trouble his nights. He observes little smiles on Stacey's lips at unexpected moments. She walks about with her head up, and looks relaxed and confident. *What's she thinking? Why the sudden change? Did someone see me with Jenna at the Holiday Inn and tell her? And why the hell would that make her happy?*

The fear Bill experiences at the thought of losing his family gnaws at his gut like a hungry rodent. Unable to break through to Stacey, he retreats to the den during the days when he isn't teaching and pretends to work on an article. He broods, and clings to Krista and Billy. *Thank God, they're too young to know what's going on.*

The last eight years of Bill's life, and his love for Stacey, loom in comparative significance to the brief, superficial indulgence he'd permitted himself. The prodigious fact that he loves his wife far beyond the mere desires of his flesh humbles Bill—and generates true shame in him for the first time.

The shame is a good start, but the dreams continue.

When he wakes in the mornings, Bill feels like he hasn't slept at all. All he remembers is the vague notion of sexual depravity involving Jenna and the prominence of her full lips and gleaming, white teeth. He also re-develops a noticeable twitch in the sagging flesh beneath his left eye—a minor affliction that has visited him at times of stress since high school. Bill has never felt worse, physically or emotionally.

⊰ 1:4 ⊱

A grey-brown December settles in Western Pennsylvania. Chilly winds threaten snow, and leafless oaks, maples, locusts, and poplars reach spiny fingers to slate skies. Stacey Miller's mien matches the grey weather, and her mood slumbers toward black December evenings.

One of the firm's private detectives had been following Bill around since the last week in November, but with nothing to report. Evidently, Bill had broken off the affair. *I didn't need a spy to tell me that. He comes home right after his classes and just about cowers at my feet.*

One evening, after another silent dinner, Bill pleads, "Stacey, I want our life back! I know I've been pre-occupied with work this semester, but I want to make it up to you."

Stacey says nothing and doesn't bother to conceal her smirk. *Pre-occupied with work. That's a good one.* She rises from the dining room table and carries Billy to the playpen in the living room. Krista—precocious as ever—watches a science channel program on the Big Bang theory. Jeff lies on the couch with his head in

Krista's lap. Stacey smiles to herself and feels content. *This is all I need, right here.*

In the kitchen, Bill is stacking dishes for washing. *Man, he really is trying. No, sorry, Bill. Doing the dishes isn't going to make up for sticking your dick in places it doesn't belong.*

"C'mon, Stacey," Bill says. "You can't keep up the cold shoulder forever." Stacey just gives him a smile and raises her eyebrows: *Wanna' bet.* She leaves the dirty dishes for him.

In the week before Christmas, Stacey drives to the law office for an appointment with Larry Rose. The white-stuccoed professional building is new. The Rose and Greenwood firm occupies the top three floors. Stacey enjoys being back in the building with its carpeted halls and windowed corner offices. When she gets off the elevator on the tenth floor, she waves at Amy through the glass wall of a conference room. Amy smiles and spreads wide her thumb and pinky next to her ear—*Call me.* Alma, Larry Rose's secretary, waves Stacey straight into Rose's office.

The office is luxurious, lined with bookshelves, and equipped with mahogany and leather furnishings. One entire wall is made of glass. The view toward the Black Moshannon Forest miles away is spectacular on this clear, December morning. Larry waves Stacey to a plush chair before a desk the size of an aircraft carrier. Stacey thinks, *In ten years, I can have an office like this.*

Larry Rose leans back in his eight hundred dollar chair and steeples his fingers on an ample stomach. "Stacey, not only as your lawyer, but as your friend, I want you to be certain this is the way forward for you. Are you sure you've thought this through?"

"Absolutely," Stacey replies without hesitation.

"Okay, fine. But the terms of the divorce will be less favorable without proof of Bill's infidelity. However, I'm nearly certain, when I steer this to the right judge, that you'll get the house and primary custody... if you're sure."

Smiling without mirth, Stacey says, "Fuck him."

No trust. No marriage.

I can't take any more of this.

Bill finally confronts Stacey in the kitchen a few days before Christmas. Fear of losing his family has been weighing him down—the veritable albatross. *Ironic, isn't it?* Bill thinks. *She should be the one confronting me. Somehow, she managed to get the shoe on the other foot.*

Bill sits in the kitchen nook. Stacey stands at the sink with her back turned to him. Snow flurries whip past the kitchen's bay window. Jim Traner across the cul-de-sac is brushing snow off his drive in a tassel hat, and predictably—for Jim—a pair of boxer shorts. The sky is slate, the light suitably dim. Jeff is sleeping next to the heat vent, his furry paws twitching as he chases a plump rabbit in his dreams. The kids are absorbed with Sponge Bob on the plasma screen television in the living room.

"For God's sake, Stacey, talk to me," he blurts. "I can't take this anymore!" Bill can feel the twitch of flesh under his eye.

Stacey turns and walks over to the nook. She slides in opposite Bill and looks him in the eye for the first time in days. He is bludgeoned by the lucidness in her brown eyes.

"I know about Jenna, Bill, so let's dispense with the bullshit." Bill literally gulps when he hears Jenna's name on his wife's lips.

He smiles a mawkish "you-caught-me-in-the-cookie-jar" grin—an involuntary reaction. Then, Stacey shoots Bill a look that pierces him like a spear point. He has a fleeting thought that he's a bug on a specimen board, and Stacey is the coldly rational entomologist.

"I'm sorry," Bill squeaks. "It's over." He looks in Stacey's eyes for as long as he can—about a half a second—and breaks into genuine, loud sobs. When he manages to get beyond his own tears and self-pity, he sees that Stacey is staring at him with a look of disgust.

"We're done, Bill," she says. "For God's sake, you fucked that little bitch in our *house*."

"No, Stacey, I never…"

"Don't even deny it," Stacey says, wagging a finger in Bill's face. "I've heard her with you in the den more than once.

"Oh, I thought you'd like to know. I found out about your little fling because some smirking asshole called and knew all about that oblong mole on the base of your cock."

Bill flinches. She'd said the word "cock" with utter contempt.

Stacey smiles at Bill, seeming to enjoy his consummate debasement. She takes another jab: "I wonder what else your little girlfriend tells him about you? Now, get the fuck out. I can't stand to look at you any longer."

⊰ 1:5 ⊱

Years later, looking back with eternal regret, Bill will remember three things vividly about the conversation that began the process that would end in divorce: Stacey's beautiful brown eyes reflecting a distance that would never be totally overcome, Jim Traner across the street shoveling snow in his ridiculous boxer shorts, and that stupid, guilty grin that betrayed him.

Bill packs a few clothes, his laptop, and a toothbrush. He moves in with Steve Lendowski, who meets him at the door of his suburban ranch style home. Shoving a beer in Bill's hand, Steve says, "Everything looks more hopeful after a Heineken. And, I think you need it, buddy." He gives Bill a slap on the back and ushers him into the living room. Jack Daniels with ice in deep glasses comes next, and by mid-afternoon, both men are comfortably drunk.

"She'll cool down," Steve says, trying to reassure Bill. "Remember, you've got history. Two kids together. A nice life. Right now, she's just thinking about making you suffer. In a couple weeks, she'll remember that you're an okay husband and a more than okay father."

"You didn't see how she looked at me this morning," Bill says. "Stacey hates my guts, and I'm not sure that I blame her."

Steve dumps the last inch of liquor into Bill's glass. "Here, drink this. It'll help you feel even sorrier for yourself. Then you can pass out and wake up as an adult."

Bill obeys. When he regains consciousness at five in the morning on Steve's couch with the worst hangover of his life, he's actually somewhat relieved. It's the first time since he'd broken it off with Jenna that he can't remember having one of those vague, but extremely unsettling, dreams.

He calls Stacey on the phone first thing. She agrees to let Bill see the kids. He spends Christmas morning opening presents with them while Stacey retreats upstairs; he does not stay for dinner. In the damp and dreary week before the New Year, she jumps in her Corolla and takes off for a couple of hours each day while Bill hangs out with Krista and Billy.

Unfiltered reality looms close as grey December afternoons quickly give way to the longest, coldest nights of the season. The nights are the worst. In the evenings, Bill drinks Jack Daniels straight from the bottle—sometimes alone, sometimes with Steve. In a cruel paradox, numbness from the whiskey brings lucidity. The situation is a disaster, and Bills knows his wife of eight years; she will divorce him, and his children will grow up in a home where he is an outsider. Still an attractive woman, Stacey may even remarry. Bill figures there is a decent chance that another man, a stranger to him, will one day play a major role in raising his children.

Depression due to his failing marriage is only one part of the malaise Bill experiences. The vaguely remembered, sexual dreams involving Jenna continue. Invariably, they engage in boisterous intercourse—of this much, Bill is certain. He remembers confiding that he misses his wife, followed by Jenna's mocking admonitions of "poor baby." In dreamland, Jenna clearly takes pleasure in having wrecked Bill's home. One morning after an especially troubling nightmare, he wakes and looks into Steve's guestroom mirror. The twitch of flesh below his left eye is more prominent. Bill thinks, *Jenna, you vindictive little cunt.*

In the most disturbing dream, Bill is involved with Jenna in an unpleasant sexual threesome. Flat on his back in a motel bed, Bill is serviced orally by Jenna. He is in ecstasy until he opens his eyes and sees a large man with dark, extremely handsome features standing at the end of the bed. There is something familiar about him. The man looks to be about forty-five, is very good-looking, and leers at Bill as he thrusts his hips rapidly in the act of penetrating Jenna from behind. The man winks and nods his head in the direction of the motel bathroom. Bill breaks away from the hauntingly familiar, grey eyes, and there's Stacey standing with crossed arms in the bathroom doorway.

After that one, Bill wakes at two a.m., sprints to Steve's guestroom toilet, and vomits.

And now, depression. The fog of Bill's thoughts is swept bare. He remains in Steve's guest bedroom for two days. Stacey and the children are set aside as the grown man of thirty-two, so pleased with himself just a few short weeks ago, curls into a mental fetal position. He can't manage to crawl out of his own misery.

Cognitive distortions frame Bill's despair. He imagines or assumes the worst possibility, then internalizes it as unequivocal fact. *Stacey will never forgive me. I'll be a stranger to my children. Stacey's lawyer will take me to the cleaners. They'll have second thoughts about me at the campus and drop me from the tenure stream.*

On New Year's Eve morning, Bill does not get out of bed. He turns his face to the wall and simply stares at a knot in the pine paneling for hours, stewing in his own misery.

Steve snaps him out of it. He pounds on the bedroom door and says, half-jokingly, half-fearfully, "Hey, man, I hope you didn't get shit all over my guestroom when you offed yourself!" He drags Bill down to the den, and provides the invalid with a healthy dose of self-medication. "Bill, my professional opinion is that you need one more gut-wrenching, all-out, brain-splitting, puke-'til-you-drop dance with Mr. Jack Daniels. Hair of the dog!"

Neither man will remember much of their conversation that evening in Steve's den, although Bill will recall, weeks later, a subsequent talk that they had when Bill finally broke free from the fetters of alcohol and depression.

On New Year's Day, Bill sleeps to five in the afternoon. After a long shower, about a gallon of ice water, and a cup of hot coffee, he feels almost human again. Steve looks refreshed in a Grateful Dead t-shirt, khaki shorts, and sandals.

"Are we ready for adulthood, now?" Steve asks cheerfully.

Steve tells Bill what he needs to hear. As a man who genuinely loves his wife and children, Bill already knows these things—but, on some level, he needs to hear the words spoken.

"You're a young man," Steve says. "And, as a young man, you have a streak of self-indulgence. After indulging yourself with

Jenna, you indulged yourself again with depression and that very ugly self-pity-party. Pathetic. I love you, man, but that shit can't go on."

Bill doesn't take offense. *How can I be offended? I know the truth when I hear it—even when it's unpleasant and extremely unflattering.*

"Let me ask you this, Bill. Do you love your wife?"

"Yes, of course," Bill replies without hesitation.

"Then you should do everything possible to reconcile." Steve ends his brief lecture with a totally insincere, "Besides, you're cramping my style here—where am I supposed to take my bitches?"

Steve's talk sets a burr under Bill's saddle. He stays busy in the two weeks before the start of the Spring semester. He visits the kids daily. There is no whiskey now, and lots of jogging.

Crossing paths with Stacey involves a perfunctory exchange of words. She dashes out the door when he comes to visit the kids. One day, Bill manages to squeeze in a few words. "I can't change what I did, Stacey. I wish I could. But I want you to know I'd do anything to make it right between us. There is nothing more important to me than you and Krista and Billy."

She doesn't say anything to that, but Bill doesn't get a letter from a divorce lawyer—yet. *At least she didn't tell me to go fuck myself.*

Feeling marginally better, Bill spends much of his time working on his lecture notes and prepping for spring classes. He feels grateful that he's lucid, and has managed to crawl out of the black hole that was his depression. On those evenings when Steve does not go out, the two men talk for hours—the campus, politics, women, and life. When there is alcohol, Heineken replaces Jack Daniels. Even the twitch below Bill's eye and the disturbing Jenna-dreams dissipate. Bill feels dispossessed, and sad, but determined to make the best of the situation.

Bill's compass needle is pointing consistently to true north. Somewhat surprised at himself, he even considers the possibility of prayer. When he was a child, his parents had occasionally taken him to the local Christian and Missionary Alliance church. But, he's thought of himself as an agnostic his entire adult life. Darwin, the military God from the Old Testament, hard science, and his natural skepticism as an academic had rendered religious faith too narrow a proposition for Bill's analytical mind, regardless of the religious seeds planted in childhood.

Oddly, it was Steve, the avowed atheist, who suggests the idea. "Bill, you need to find the source of your inner strength and use it. Have you considered prayer?"

They're sharing a pizza for dinner, and Bill almost chokes on a slice as they sit in Steve's living room. *You've got to be fucking kidding me.* Bill gives Steve a glance brimming with incredulity.

Responding with a little shrug, Steve says, "Hey, it worked for the Children of Israel in Egypt."

"Yeah, right," Bill snorts. "And the Crusaders, and those warm, fuzzy characters responsible for the Spanish Inquisition. Oh, right, and let's not forget al-Qaeda. Faith in God is producing some really lovely outcomes there.

"Shit, man, prayer at this time in my life would be like a convict 'finding God' in maximum security. No atheists in foxholes, right? I'd feel like a fool and a hypocrite."

"Methinks thou doth protest too much," Steve says. "Maybe you should give it a try. Even if the Big-Guy-in-the-Sky isn't up there, the possibility alone might give you a boost. Or, you could try meditation. Whatever works for you, man."

Bill shrugs and doesn't respond. Steve changes the subject to the new Harper Lee prequel coming out. Bill doesn't listen because he's preoccupied by Steve's unexpected suggestion. *A little Divine Intervention wouldn't hurt.* Bill remembers the inner voice that spoke to him that last time in the office with Jenna and the night he took a good look at his children for the first time in weeks: *Remember what's important.*

One frosty morning after the new year, Bill jogs down the road, thinking, *Oh, what the hell—it can't hurt.* Feeling awkward and self-conscious, Bill prays. He acknowledges the wrongfulness of his adultery. Exhaled air puffs out in little white clouds when he says aloud, "Please, God, let Stacey forgive me."

Bill feels better after that—like a weight has been lifted from his shoulders. He is not prepared to say whether the comfort the prayer brings is derived from a "Higher Source," or is due to some self-made psychological construct. *One thing's for sure,* he thinks, *it's the first time in weeks I've had more than a glimmer of hope. Who knows? Maybe she'll take me back.*

Remember what's important.

⚜ 1:6 ⚜

Bill's knees buckle when Stacey agrees to think over giving him another chance. A part of him had doubted that reconciliation was a possibility.

"We'll see, Bill. Give me a month. I'm pissed."

When she hangs up the phone, Bill breathes a prayer of thanks.

Bill doesn't push Stacey. He'll give her the month. Meanwhile, he runs, lifts weights at the campus gym, and works on his lecture notes. He also prays, which continues to give him a feeling of hope. The disturbing dreams about Jenna have faded. Even the eye twitch reverts to its infrequent norm.

Only one rather peculiar incident mars what Bill thinks of as progress during the last days in early January before classes start.

One morning, jogging on the rural lane that runs past Steve's house and down to the campus outside of town, Bill sees Jenna with her arms around a guy on a motorcycle. It's a nice bike, a Harley with loud pipes. Driving the mean looking machine is a man who looks familiar. *Where do I know this guy from?*

The motorcycle slows and comes to a crawl right next to Bill.

What the hell is this? Neither rider wears a helmet, so Bill can clearly see the wicked pleasure on Jenna's face when she reaches around and grabs her new lover's crotch. Bill feels an unexpected sting of jealousy. Jenna gives him a finger-wiggle-little-girl-wave and that lascivious smile he remembers so well.

Next comes the real weirdness, what Bill will later think of as his "Stephen-King-moment." The man, who looks so familiar, winks at Bill. A *forked tongue* shoots out of his mouth and flicks down past the bottom of his chin.

The bike tears off down the road, leaving behind a cloud of blue smoke and a black trail of rubber.

What the fuck? That TONGUE. Bill had seen something like it on MSNBC or Dateline—weirdoes who sliced their tongues with a razor blade. *Supposedly, a cunnilingus aid, but more likely a "hey-look-at-me-I'm-a-freak" fashion statement,* Bill surmises.

He tries to laugh it off, but can't help feeling uneasy. Later that morning when he shaves after a shower, Bill notices the twitch of flesh beneath his left eye has returned.

All that day, Bill works in Steve's home office, so busy he doesn't even think about the incident again until that night in bed. Steve is out late with some graduate student, and the house is full of unfamiliar night sounds. Just as sleep closes in, Bill sits straight up in the bed. His forearms break out in gooseflesh. He remembers how he knows the guy on the Harley. Jenna's new boyfriend is the man from Bill's sexual threesome dream—the one where Stacey was watching.

Bill jumps out of the bed and turns on a light. He hurries down to the kitchen in his boxers, turning on every light along the way. Steve still has not come home. Bill grabs a beer from the fridge and chugs it down. About halfway through the second one, he sits at the kitchen table and loses the urge to keep glancing over his shoulder. He runs over the incident in his mind.

Must have been a trick of my eyes—the length of the tongue. But the sudden appearance of a character from a dream—that's fucking weird! There must be a rational explanation. I probably saw the guy around the campus and inserted him into my dream as real-life residue. Then, presto!, there he is, hauling around my ex-girlfriend in the waking world. Yeah, that's it. He's a new staffer at Glenville—maintenance, maybe—and now he's drilling Jenna. Probably the same asshole that called Stacey with the good news.

Over the next few days, Bill dismisses Jenna and her new lover as harmless freaks. The strangeness of the episode even helps Bill to distance himself from his extra-marital fling, and bolsters his view of himself as a good person. His affair with Jenna had been an aberration, as he surely did not belong in the same category with a man that mutilates his tongue and drives a Harley in the middle of a Western Pennsylvania winter.

Turning his attention to what he thinks are more immediate concerns, Bill polishes his lectures and thinks about how to repair the damage to his marriage. The question of whether Jenna and her new boyfriend might be truly dangerous never crosses his mind.

Part II

The Man in the Meadow

Tyka snatches up a groundhog and scarfs it down in two gulps. A black bear and her three cubs saunter past. The coyotes keep their distance, and are even helpful, scaring up game as they do. Tyka reigns supreme. The smell of man remains distant, far removed on the other side of the river. She wishes for her mate, but comes to understand that this is unrelated to her purpose.

The nights grow longer. Tyka hunts and feeds on the plentiful game. Winds from the northwest deliver a refreshing chill to the forest. Tyka becomes restless and howls from time to time. She is lonely.

A new smell pervades the forest. Tyka pursues its source and discovers a moss-encrusted cabin. The shanty appears to be abandoned, but the smell of a human—or something like a human—is robust. Tyka returns to the area of the cabin repeatedly over the ensuing weeks.

One evening, she spots a woman gliding through the trees. Tyka freezes like a statute in mid-trot. It is the Tunku—the master. The one who called her far from the north and set within her sinews a sense of self-awareness and purpose. Tyka is drawn to her, but intuits that she will call, or summon her, when the time is right. Tyka waits.

When the wolf sleeps, she begins to dream of a human family. There are two adults and two smaller offspring. A kindred spirit is among them, though it is much weaker—almost pathetic. The humans and the "dog" are in some kind of brightly lit cave. A voice in the dream speaks to Tyka, and says, "This is your purpose."

When she wakes beneath a rock overhang deep in the Black

Moshannon, Tyka finds that she has been imbued with a strong desire. She has never tasted it, but somehow understands that what she experiences is a craving for human muscle, bone, and blood.

The leaves fall from many of the trees and blanket the forest floor with a brown shroud. Tyka becomes frightened when a man joins the woman in the cabin. His smell is unique and dangerous. Tyka resolves to avoid this creature.

After the season's first arctic air mass settles over the region, the winds shift to the east and become damp with moisture. Wind-swept snow blankets the forest with a heavy shroud. Tyka makes her way back to the cabin through drifts that rise above her shoulders. As she approaches the shack, she smells the man and a different female. The strange man wades through the snow with a woman slung over one shoulder. He carries the limp form into the cabin. Tyka thinks of the family she dreams about, and intuits a command from the Tunku: WAIT.

The master emerges from the shanty and approaches Tyka. She tosses the wolf a large hunk of dripping meat. It is a human arm that has been torn loose from the shoulder socket.

She devours the warm flesh and crunches the bones as the Tunku strokes her ears. "Soon," the woman—who is not really a woman—promises Tyka.

⊰ 2:1 ⊱

The grey new year in Western Pennsylvania reflects different realities for Bill and Stacey Miller. Bill gravitates steadily toward a more peaceful state of mind and fully accepts the consequences of his actions. He is still a "Doubting Thomas," but can't deny that a mustard seed of faith, sown in his youth, has somehow sprouted and borne fruit. Bill prays, and thinks, *God is in control. If I trust Him, everything will be okay.*

Stacey does not have the consolation of faith and long ago set aside her deceased father's Catholicism. And, just when she'd accepted her marriage as a failed enterprise—had actually finalized the paperwork to inform Bill of her intention to divorce him—Stacey again finds herself at a place of indecision. She finally turns to her mother for advice.

"So, you think I should let him get away with it? I don't know if I can do that, Mom." Stacey is surprised to be having this conversation with her mother. *She's never been a fan of Bill. And, now, she's telling me to take him back. What gives?*

"Stacey, dear, I'm not going to sugarcoat this," Isabella says, leaning back in the living room's recliner with a noticeable wince. Stacey raises her eyebrows and begins to speak, but her mother cuts her off. "It's pride, dear. You're making a decision that will impact not only you, but your *children* for the rest of your lives. And, you're making that decision based on your damaged ego. I think you're making a mistake."

Stacey opens her mouth to start an argument, then snaps it shut with an audible click. This is her mother's apartment, and Stacey thinks it would be more than disrespectful to dismiss her viewpoint without considering it. *Besides, she has a point. I couldn't see it, though, until she said it.*

Stacey checks out the plethora of pill bottles on the coffee table. *And what's with that grimace? She looks like she's in pain.*

"Mom, it's more than my pride. I don't know if I can forgive him. And how can you have a marriage without trust?"

"You don't have to forgive him, or trust him," Isabella replies, shifting uncomfortably in the recliner. "And you don't have to let him *get away with it*, as you put it. Don't forget. Now that you've caught him, you have the upper hand. Bill still loves you, and it would be no shame on you if you used his affair against him. No more fifty-fifty, Stacey. Bill sacrificed that, and he knows it.

"Honey, Bill's a good man who fell into a trap. You're not the first woman it's happened to."

Stacey doesn't say anything. She absently strokes the grey fur on Smokey, Isabella's fat old tomcat. Wounded pride and ego aside, part of Stacey hates herself for embracing her mother's unexpected words. To take Bill back reeks of weakness, a trait she has strenuously avoided since childhood. All through the marriage she's felt like her part has been one of deference, and here it is again—the actual contemplation of letting the son-of-a-bitch slide.

After some minutes, Stacey looks up quickly as if waking from a reverie. Her mother is eyeing her across the coffee table lined with bottles of prescription medication.

"What's going on, Mom?" Stacey asks. "And don't bullshit me. I know you're sick."

Isabella sighs. Stacey thinks she sees a momentary watering of her mother's eyes, but it passes quickly. *She looks so frail. My God—it's serious.*

"I'm sorry, baby," Isabella says. "It's terminal. Stage four pancreatic cancer. I'll be gone before the snow melts."

Stacey endures the twenty-four hours after her mother's revelation in turmoil. She cares for the kids in a distracted fog and grits her teeth when the idea of calling Bill automatically enters her mind. *Just when I get up from a punch in the nose, I get hammered with a kick to the gut. And my first reaction is to turn to the guy who gave me the punch in the nose? C'mon, Stacey, suck it up!*

Stacey paces the linoleum in the kitchen at midnight. She asks the question millions have asked when misfortune drops by for an extended visit: *Why me?*

An epiphany hits Stacey like a shovel to the face. She stops pacing back and forth abruptly. *I've been feeling sorry for myself. Damn. It's not all about me, is it?*

She doesn't waste any time on shame—another self-indulgence.

By three a.m., Stacey has it figured out.

"Oh, my God, Stacey, I'm so sorry." Amy, deeply concerned, reaches across the table in a corner of the Starbucks and squeezes Stacey's hand.

Stacey looks down and inhales an uneven breath. A single tear strikes the slate-colored tabletop.

"Thanks, Amy," Stacey says, looking up and giving her friend a brave smile. "I was going to bust if I didn't find a sympathetic ear."

"What can I do, sweetie? I'll watch the brats. Anything."

Stacey chuckles—"Aunt" Amy has been a regular babysitter, and the kids love her. *She seems a bit distracted today, though. Glancing around all the time like she's expecting someone. But, here she is the minute I pick up the phone.*

"Being here and listening is plenty," Stacey replies. "You're a true friend."

Amy nods with furrowed brow. "So, what's next?" she asks. "Hospice?"

"Mom has it set up, but that's not how it's going to happen. She'll fight me tooth and nail, but she's coming to live with me and Bill."

Amy raises her eyebrows and shoots Stacey a questioning look.

After a moment, Stacey realizes what she has said. "Right, I forgot to mention it, didn't I? Don't fall off your chair, Amy. I'm giving Bill another chance."

"Are you sure, Stace? Maybe this isn't the best time to make that kind of decision. You could just keep things in a holding pattern for a while."

Stacey sighs, says, "No, I'm as sure of this as when I agreed to marry him. The thing is, Amy, my mother was right about me. I was determined to divorce Bill because my pride was wounded, and I wanted payback."

"And trust?"

"Trust and forgiveness are secondary," Stacey replies firmly. "Last night I asked myself, 'What's the best thing to do?' The answer is clear: keep my family together.

"You didn't see Krista's face when she told me she missed having her father around the house as much as he was before. And, do you know what Billy's first full sentence was? He said, 'Where's da-da, mum-mum, where's da-da?'"

"But is it right for *you*, Stacey? You count too, you know?"

"I'm secondary, too, Amy. And, the thing is, I still love the jerk. This whole thing—it's just not who Bill really is. I honestly think the affair was an aberration. That's no excuse, but it does mean something."

Amy reaches across the table and gives Stacey's hand another squeeze. She smiles, and says, "Whatever you need, Stacey. I'm here for you."

They change the subject from death and divorce to Amy. She tells Stacey that when June arrives she will be a grandmother. They joke and laugh a little about the "hottest-grandmother-this-side-of-the-Little-Kittaning-River," and then the sound of a motorcycle tearing out of the parking lot makes Amy jump.

"What's wrong?" Stacey asks. "You've seemed a little nervy all morning."

Amy waves a hand dismissively and shakes her head. "Oh, it's nothing serious, I'm sure. I wasn't going to say anything with all your troubles, but I think I have a stalker."

"Jesus, Amy, what's going on?"

Amy laughs, but Stacey thinks it's the most nervous laugh she's ever heard.

"I don't think it's a big deal," Amy says. "That waitress that disappeared last week has me a little spooked, I guess. They didn't report it in the news, but you know we hear things in the office. Apparently, she was snatched right out of her car—in her own driveway.

"Anyhow, I probably wouldn't have noticed this guy at all, except for how he looks. This is the weird part. The first time I saw him in the strip mall across from the law office, I thought it was your husband."

"That's odd. Are you sure it wasn't actually Bill?"

"No, this guy is definitely older than Bill. I'm sure it's just a coincidence, anyhow. Glenville isn't exactly a metropolis. I probably noticed this guy because of how much he resembles Bill, and now I just see him around."

Stacey thinks Amy doesn't sound totally convinced. *She's not telling me everything.* "Okay, but don't mess around," Stacey says. "You still carry that .38 in your purse? Good. And call me so I don't worry!"

When they rise to leave, Amy and Stacey hug.

"Anything you need, you hear me?"

"Thanks, Amy."

When his wife calls him on his cell and says, "It's time to come home," Bill falls down on his knees in the middle of Steve's study and thanks God. That Stacey wants him back seems like nothing less than a miracle.

"She's giving me another chance," he tells Steve, who gives Bill a slap on the back on his way out the door.

"Now, don't screw it up," Steve yells good-naturedly as Bill jogs to his car in the drive.

Motoring home, he sees the traffic on a subconscious level. Bill realizes the reconciliation will not be a simple matter. *This is going to be awkward. I'll be on probation—maybe indefinitely.*

A shameful grin twitches the side of Bill's mouth when he saunters through the front door without knocking. A thought races through his mind: *I got away with it.* It's gone in a flash. Bill knows that the unwelcome thought is not who he is. "I'm home," he calls, and that sounds very right.

When Stacey greets him in the living room, Bill sees that some of the distance is gone from her eyes. He falls on his knees and hugs her legs.

Stacey despises the weakness she sees in her husband and can't help but feel superior. She thinks, *This is going to take some work.*

They walk on eggshells that first day. Bill spends most of the time with Big Billy rolling around on the floor, and then with Krista, home from morning kindergarten. Jeff jumps about the frolicking threesome and barks happily. They watch a lot of Sponge Bob. Stacey orders out for pizza.

The couple makes love later that night for the first time in months. For Bill, it's like "coming home" all over again. He tells Stacey this, but she rolls over with her back to him. Bill snuggles against her, wraps his arm around her waist, and holds on tight. He does not see her tears as Stacey weeps in silence.

Bill will not find out until later how much has been lost—a fact that now hits Stacey like a whirlwind.

Of course things will never be the same, she thinks. *How could it be otherwise?*

⚜ 2:2 ⚜

In the first week after kindergarten starts in January, Krista gets off the school bus, walks into the house, and finds her father playing with Billy on the living room floor. She's surprised because this is not his usual time to visit.

"Come here, Krista," her dad says, suddenly very serious. She walks over to him, and he grabs her and starts tickling. For some minutes the three of them just roll around on the floor, laughing. Jeff, his tail wagging furiously, joins the fun.

Bill stops fooling around and props himself in a sitting position against the couch. He sits Krista down in front of him and looks deep into her big brown eyes, so much like Stacey's. "Sweetie," he says, "I'm going to be home all the time now."

Krista wants to hope, but she is troubled. The five year old prodigy frowns. After a minute, she finally asks, "Is it forever?"

Bill pulls Krista to his chest and hugs her tight. She does not see his tears.

"Yeah, baby," Bill croaks in a low, broken voice. "I'll never leave you again."

Krista's mom orders pizza. As they sit around the dining room table eating, Krista dares to hope that they will be a happy family again.

Stacey doesn't join them after dinner when Krista, Bill, and Billy watch old VHS tapes of the Bugs Bunny/Road Runner show. Jeff curls up against Krista on the couch and sleeps with his head in her lap. Krista feels happy for the first time in months.

That night, she has difficulty sleeping after her daddy tucks her under the bed covers. She thinks back over the last several months and resists the urge to suck her thumb. *I'm not a baby like Billy.* Billy is going through the TERRIBLE TWOS—she's heard her mom and Grammy Issy talking about the toddler's piercing, screaming fits. Krista had relished her role as Big-Sister-Protector, but lately she'd become annoyed with "the brat."

As she drifts toward sleep, her mind turns to other, more pressing concerns. Krista thinks, *I wish the man in the backyard would go away.*

The beginning of kindergarten was one of the happiest times of Krista's young life. Mrs. Artis, most of the kids, and the brightly colored classroom quickly diminished Krista's initial anxiety about leaving home for half the day. But, then, something happened that scared her so badly she had to go talk to a doctor.

During that twilight stage between waking and full sleep, people sometimes experience visual illusions. Little Krista saw a disembodied face hovering over her bed. Her mother's face. It smiled with unmistakable malice. Krista realized it wasn't her mother at all—it was something *imitating* her mother. Krista shrieked, and seconds later, her mom and dad burst into the bedroom to comfort her.

Doctor Adams called it "night terrors," a fairly common occurrence in children, probably derived from suppressed anxiety due to starting kindergarten. Krista did not understand all of this, but she heard the doctor assure her parents that it probably would not recur.

Then, her father moved out of the house.

Krista was forced to accommodate feelings and circumstances many adults failed to successfully negotiate. She never did believe her parents' lie that Bill had to work more. *They don't have school at night,* she scoffed to herself. Krista was miffed that, whatever the reason for Bill's departure, her mother and father did not trust her with the truth.

Imbued with uncommon intelligence, the child of five began to perceive the sordid reality that defines humankind. Krista was unable to put her feelings into words—did not have the vocabulary for what were quite sophisticated thoughts—and that frustrated her. She remained unhappy and anxious much of the time.

In the week before her dad came home to stay, Krista's anxiety blossomed into terror.

A man stood in the field of weeds behind the house at night and stared at her window. The first time she saw him, he was only a dark shadow in the silver moonlight. She'd awakened for no apparent reason, walked to her bedroom window, and there he was, about fifty yards from the house standing motionless in the middle of the fallow meadow. Krista rubbed her eyes to clear the sleep from them. She stared out the window for five minutes.

The man never moved. Convincing herself that it was some trick of the moonlight, Krista went back to bed.

Every night after that, as the moon waxed, Krista woke and looked out to see the man. And, each time, he stood closer to the house. By the fourth night—after the big snow—he was at the border where the field of weeds and thistles became the smooth, white expanse of the Millers' back yard. The silver-white light was much stronger by then, and Krista could see that he wasn't just looking at the house—*he was staring directly up at her bedroom window.* That night Jeff slunk from her bedroom and would not return.

The next day, Krista's forehead felt warm. Her mom made her stay home from school. Krista didn't tell her mother about the man in the backyard. She figured Stacey wouldn't believe her and would make her go back to Dr. Adams.

By mid-morning, Krista grew tired of reading a Nancy Drew and popped in a DVD of *Planet Earth: From Pole to Pole*. With Stacey in the kitchen and Billy napping, the house was far too quiet without some kind of background noise.

A few minutes into the documentary, movement out of the corner of her eye made Krista jump. She jerked her head. A formless shadow flitted up the steps to the second floor. Krista's forearms broke out in gooseflesh. She turned off the TV and listened.

There was no sound. Nothing. Not even the tick of the grandfather clock. Krista wanted to call for her mother but couldn't find the breath to form words. She fought her body's attempted betrayal—the urge to pee. Finally, sound slowly returned. She heard the blood coursing through the miniature liquid highways in her ears; the clock tick-tick-ticked; a bird twittered outside the bay window.

Krista heaved a sigh, but peed herself a little when a very loud engine, probably a motorcycle, revved up right in front of the house.

Stacey said, "Fucking morons," from the kitchen. The spell broke, and Krista was not bothered at all by the fact that her mother would curse loud enough for her daughter to hear.

That night, when Krista woke up and looked out her window, the man was standing in the yard by the swing-set. The moonlight made his eyes shine. A long dark thing—what must have been his tongue—flicked out inches below his chin. In the five minutes that Krista stared, terrified but partially mesmerized, his tongue never stopped flicking, in and out.

The next day, Krista's dad came home to stay.

Krista wakes around two-thirty in the morning. She thinks of her father in the house at night for the first time in six weeks, but she is not comforted. She feels compelled to get out of bed and look out the window.

I should tell Daddy about the man. But, what if he thinks it's the night terrors? What if he doesn't believe me? He might get upset and leave again! Krista's heart knows that her father would not willingly leave her, but the irrational fear gnaws at her nonetheless.

Krista fights the urge to get out of bed. She loses the battle and casts aside the bedclothes. A white shaft of moonlight blazes a path across the floor. The hardwood is cold under her feet as she takes reluctant baby steps toward the window. She can hear Jeff whimpering downstairs.

I don't wanna' look; I don't wanna' look; I don't wanna' look.

Krista looks.

The backyard is empty. For the first time in a week, the man is not staring up at her. Krista lets out her breath in a big *whoosh*.

The backyard and the fallow meadow beyond it are bathed in glorious, white light. The swing set casts a dark shadow on the rapidly melting snow. *It's so bright; I could go out on the patio and read a book.*

Krista turns away with a sigh. Her eye catches movement outside the window. She turns back.

Two large hands grip the brick sill on the other side of the glass.

A dark figure pulls itself up until its head and shoulders are above the sill. Krista stares into familiar grey eyes from a distance of six inches. A forked tongue shoots out and flicks against the window with a soft thump.

Krista screams.

"His eyes! His eyes! *I know his eyes!*"

⚜ 2:3 ⚜

Across the small college town, about three miles as the wolf runs, the wind whips through the Glenville campus. The cloudless January night allows the glowing moon to cast moving shadows of the naked oaks and maples, waving spiny fingers at no one. The rising wind produces a low moan—an empty sound devoid of soul or feeling.

The campus is deserted. The spring semester starts late at Glenville, and students are not permitted to move back into the dorms for another two days. At three in the morning, the small university is served by a skeleton crew of two security guards, who forego hourly patrols for the warmth of the security office. The force is one guard short, as the latest hire, twenty-three year old Pete Dorgan, has been a no show/no call since the week before Christmas.

Inside the Boyle dormitory, a grey mouse hurries down the recently buffed corridor of the third floor. Shifting moonlight moves across the tile of the darkened hall. The only other light shines dimly from two red EXIT signs at either end. The mouse easily slips under the door of room 3E and enters an apartment built for three students.

The mouse cares nothing for the room, or the figure of a young woman stretched back on a recliner in the darkened common area of the apartment. Ignoring the soft moaning, the rodent is drawn to the treat in the bathroom. It skitters over a newspaper strewn on the carpeted floor and produces a subtle rustle when it crosses a headline that reads, "Five Month Old Infant Raped by Glenville Man."

If the mouse could read, or cared about such things, it might have looked to the next page to read an article about a woman who'd spent the entirety of the last two years sitting on a toilet. Authorities, called to a rural trailer home by neighbors complaining about barking dogs and a stench, were forced to call paramedics and a surgeon to remove the woman—her flesh and muscle tissue had grown around the toilet seat. The article didn't mention that the unfortunate woman's boyfriend, who'd brought her food to keep her alive, also penetrated her orally, on a daily basis, as she sat on the commode.

The little grey mouse is not interested in the fact that a five month old infant required multiple surgical procedures to repair her damaged insides; that as paramedics removed the baby from the home, she swallowed her little tongue and almost choked to death; that the woman on the toilet consented to everything; or, that the woman on the recliner—Jenna—read of these events and responded to the knowledge as if she'd been exposed to a powerful aphrodisiac. No, the mouse is not interested in Jenna or the depravities of the public at large. Instead, it scurries to the unusual meal awaiting it in the apartment's bathroom.

The rodent, whiskers twitching, hurries across the tile floor and climbs the vinyl shower curtain decorated with a tropical sunset. In the tub is a ripening corpse. The mouse scampers across the body in anticipation.

Scooting across a silver nameplate which reads, PETE DOR-GAN, SECURITY OFFICER, the mouse makes for an eyeball lying on the mannequin-like face. The eye is still connected by the optic nerve. The mouse nibbles at the absolutely delicious flesh in the back cavity, rich with *vitreous humor* and blood vessels. If one cares to listen, one might hear the tiny chewing and tearing sounds the mouse makes as it dines.

In the next room, Jenna is taking her time, moaning and writh-ing on the recliner as she inserts a large pointed object into her vagina. The room is almost completely dark, and the rising wind joins its atonal howl to the primal moan Jenna emits.

A scud of cloud exits from the face of the moon. Pale white light from the window glints off the object Jenna uses to pleasure herself. It is an icicle removed from the dorm's eave.

The mouse does not comprehend the strangeness of all this; nor, if it had cared to look, would it have been troubled by the observation that even when Jenna finishes with the spike of ice and tosses it carelessly aside, the object remains frosty and dry, with no evidence of melting. Only after an hour passes, but dawn yet remains a distant blemish on the glorious night, do a few drops of melting water appear on the surface of the icicle as it lay in the heated apartment.

Meanwhile, the mouse, oblivious to human (and inhuman) de-pravity, nibbles some more.

Three miles from the campus, as a momentarily satiated Jenna reclines, and the mouse devours Pete Dorgan's eyeball, Jeff, the Millers' black lab, cowers behind the living room sofa. In Jeff's canine mind and soul lurks a growing sense of approaching danger—a foreboding derived from a sensory perception as yet undiscovered by science, related to scent, and enhanced by reflected moonlight.

Jeff whines and squirts a little pee by accident. The danger comes from a man in the backyard. But it's not really a man—doesn't smell like one at all. Jeff can sense rage and lust emanating from it, but he is too frightened to bark or howl. The dog is protective of his masters—who he thinks of as *Tunku*—but fear nearly overwhelms love and duty.

Jeff whimpers softly, and passes into an uneasy sleep where his dreams are no longer filled with the rabbit in the backyard and the rubber ball the girl *Tunku* throws for him. In his dog dream, Jeff follows the scent of the adult male *Tunku* through a vast forest. The master is pursued by the thing in the backyard, but Jeff is no longer afraid. He will rend the man-who-is-not-a-man with his powerful jaws and save the master. The chase comes to an end, however, when Jeff arrives at a nearly vertical cliff that drops dozens of feet to a raging torrent. The smell of a great fire wafts across the river too swift and turbulent to cross. A wolf howls.

Jeff wakes suddenly, and his hackles rise. The young female *Tunku* screams in her upstairs bedroom.

⚒ 2:4 ⚒

Seven weeks after Stacey kicked Bill out of the house, they are back in the breakfast nook. Unlike that morning, this January day is unusually warm. Two feet of snow buried Glenville just two days previous, but now a mild wind from the south rapidly melts it. The morning is so mild that Jim Traner in his boxer shorts across the cul-de-sac doesn't seem so strange.

Stacey has made bacon and eggs in silence. She puts two full plates on the table and sits down across from Bill.

Embarrassed and feeling unnatural, Bill asks, "Will you forgive me, Stacey?" Bill knows that the issue is very much undecided in her mind, the previous night's lovemaking aside. He feels the distance between them more than ever as she stares out the window in silence.

Seconds stretch out like minutes. Stacey sighs, then says, "Let's give it some time, Bill."

He notes that she calls him Bill, not "Billy," as was her custom. *Maybe her forgiving me won't be the hardest part. A more critical issue may be whether or not she'll TRUST me again.*

More unnatural quiet settles over the kitchen like a cloud. Just to say something, Stacey says, "What the hell's going on with Jeff? If he pees on the rug again, he'd better get used to the backyard."

"I guess he'll have to sleep in the basement if he keeps it up," Bill replies, happy to change the subject. After a moment, he continues with a more pressing issue: "Do you think it's the night terrors again?"

The previous night, Krista woke them at three a.m. with a shrill scream. No amount of prodding could elicit an explanation from the hysterical girl. They allowed Krista to sleep in their bed and decided to let her stay home from school. She still sleeps as they sit in the kitchen.

Stacey takes her plate to the sink. With her back turned to Bill, she replies, "Her Daddy moved out of the house this Christmas. It wasn't hard on just you and me."

Bill thinks, *bitch*, and just as quickly repents. He rightly suffers at the thought of emotional damage to Krista precipitated in some measure by his lust, but still feels bitter that Stacey would so readily pierce him with that particular dagger—and twist. He represses the human urge to defend himself and absorbs the jab. *Hell, I deserve it—and more.*

Scraping the remnants of breakfast from her plate, Stacey feels that she may have a lifetime of daggers stored up. She thinks about last night when she'd lain beside Bill with wide eyes staring at the ceiling long after he'd commenced snoring. *Blaming Bill for Krista's episode is unfair and vindictive. I need to put his affair behind us. I chose to live with him again, so it's not really fair to be a total bitch about it.*

Bill takes his plate to the sink and pauses beside her. She turns her cheek up to him, and he kisses it.

"We gonna' be okay, babe?" Bill asks.

Stacey manufactures a little smile for Bill's benefit and deflects the topic away from their relationship. "I'm worried about Amy," she says. "She hasn't answered her cell or returned my calls for three days."

"Maybe she ran off with Dr. Phil," Bill quips.

Stacey emits a forced laugh despite her genuine concern for Amy. She says, "Asshole," and gives Bill a half-hearted jab with her elbow in his chiseled midsection. She becomes serious quickly. "I mean it. She said she thought some guy might be stalking her."

"Oh." Bill sobers. "Why don't you call the law office? I'm sure she's fine. This up and down weather gets everybody sick.

"Anyhow, gotta' go or I'll be late the first day of classes. I have to drop by Steve's for my laptop first. I'll give you a call around lunch."

Bill gives Stacey another peck, lifts Billy out of the playpen to blow a raspberry on his stomach, and takes off.

Backing out of the driveway and leaving the cul-de-sac behind, Bill is absorbed by what he has done—the pain he has caused. *Stacey's distance in bed last night was not good. I'm going to have to work overtime at this. I owe her that.*

Driving to Steve's house, Bill experiences intrusive flashes—thoughts of sex with Jenna. The memories arouse him. The capricious wind driving his thoughts raises an image of Krista from the night before, tearful and frantic. Bill's heart breaks from love and concern. Flaming lust turns to dead ash. *I am such a fucking scumbag. I WILL make this right!*

Bill doesn't see the suburban homes he passes, and is only sub-consciously aware of stopping at traffic lights and washing bug guts (*bugs in January?*) off the windshield. His thoughts scurry in all directions like frightened vermin that can't decide how to escape a sinking ship. He thinks of Steve with his laid-back 1960s out-look—a true friend who talked, drank, joked, and smoked pot through the roughest month of Bill's life. A sudden cerebral gust sends the course of his mind in a different direction, and Bill spends some pleasant minutes in "escape mode," dwelling on mundane items like his spring courses, class rosters, departmental politics, and syllabi.

The winds shift again and gradually rise into a constant force that flows in one direction, sure and true. The pavement of the road passes by unseen. The unusually mild, late January day—warm enough to trick insects into hatching—is an afterthought requiring little attention. A loud motorcycle flies past going the opposite direction, and Bill barely notices. He sees his wife's eyes absent some of the distance, his lovely and bright daughter laugh-ing at cartoons, and his toddler son taking shaky steps with a look of mixed fear and determination on his chubby face.

As certainly as fickle winds in a storm push a flag first one way, then another, before the prominent force sets the cloth straight and true in a single direction, so too, over the course of the ride across town, Bill's mind settles on a singular, unwavering thought.

Everything is going to be okay.

Bill will remember the moment for a long time. He will even question whether there actually had been a voice from outside him—the words are *that* real. This wind is sure and true, does not falter, and, unlike Bill's fickle compass needle, blows true north. He recalls his re-discovered faith, and it fills him with joy.

Pulling into the driveway of Steve's ranch house sitting alone between the town of Glenville and the campus of Glenville State University, it occurs to Bill with perfect lucidity that his slip with Jenna may have been, in some mysterious way, *absolutely necessary.*

The wind is blowing dead ahead—perfect for sailing to a far off but reachable land of plenty. Whatever storms may come, be it divorce or child psychiatry, Bill, wrapped in a cocoon of well-being not of his making (or so he believes), is confident he will steer a straight course.

As a wind of hurricane proportions nears, Bill fills with hope. He strides to Steve's front stoop with a feeling of peace.

Steve's front door has been shattered to splinters. *The door looks like someone went at it with a hundred pound sledgehammer.* Bill thinks of the cell phone in his Subaru, but is drawn through the remnants of the door and into the house. *I have to see.*

The foyer tiled with artificial stone and the hall leading back to the bedrooms reveal no horrors. Bill ignores the hallway and glides into the living room. He is unaware of sound or the passage of time. He does not feel the carpeted floor beneath him. Nothing seems real. The sense of empowerment from faith in God has vanished like chaff in a storm.

Bill's feet move him forward, but it's like being on a conveyer belt which slowly, but inexorably, transports him to some horrible doom. The back of his neck tickles. *He's behind me.* Bill whirls around. The living room—empty. Through the splintered door, his dark green Subaru sits behind Steve's Volvo in the sunlit drive.

Bill turns in slow motion and continues through the preternaturally quiet house. He halts at the entrance to the home's kitchen like he walked into a closed door.

Steve sits at the round kitchen table. He is naked except for scarlet-stained boxer shorts on the floor around his ankles. His open eyes cap a surprised expression. A large incision from his sternum to his scrotum gapes wide open. Ropes of grey intestine coil in a heap on the table. An out-of-place January blowfly, all alone, alights and lands on the pile of guts.

Bill pisses himself. Coherent thought flees to some dark corner of his mind. The ebb and flow of the wind that had sailed his thoughts on the car ride over to Steve's has spawned a tempest where lucidity is swept bare.

The image sears into the tissue of Bill's brain. He will never forget the spreading pool of blood on the tiled floor, the blowfly, or the mound of grey intestines sliced from the belly of the man who'd been a great friend and mentor.

Bill screams loudly, three times. It is not a high, shrill scream, but deep and masculine—full of outrage, anguish, and anger. He backs out of the kitchen and stumbles across the living room to the demolished front door.

Wanting to look behind but unable to, Bill walks quickly with a stiff-legged gait to his car—and drops his keys. Two thoughts occur: *That blood was fresh; he's behind me with a scalpel.* Bill emits a frightened yelp and whirls around. Sunlight dazzles his eyes. The shattered door yawns on the relatively dark interior where anyone or anything might suddenly emerge.

A maniac does not dash out the door as Bill fumbles in the driveway with his keys. He grips them, opens the car door, and hits his head on the roof as he climbs behind the wheel. *Lock the doors! Lock the doors!* He locks the car's doors and snatches his Blackberry from the passenger seat.

Bill stares blankly at the cell phone. He can't remember the number one calls in an emergency. He jerks his head up to look at the broken door of the house—still no maniac. Bill's fingers tingle. The quick, labored gasps of what sounds like a lunatic resound through the interior compartment of the car. *I'm hyperventilating. Get a grip!*

An insane memory, unbidden, fills up Bill's consciousness: Sponge Bob and Patrick (in fishnet stockings) are on a mission to save Bikini Bottom. The memory has nothing to do with anything, but it causes Bill to think of his daughter. The cartoon memory and thoughts of Krista are replaced with a vivid image of Jenna on the back of a chopper, riding *bitch* to a forty-something guy with a forked tongue (who looks so *very* familiar).

9-1-1. It's *9-1-1, you dope.* Bill taps the cell phone screen without making a mistake.

"9-1-1, what's your emergency?"

"I, I, um... FUCK!"

Bill can't remember Steve's address, or his own. Frustration, fear, and panic rise to new heights, and crazily, Bill's misfiring brain summons a vision, unbidden to be sure, of an unseen figure screwing off the top of his head and stirring the contents inside the skull with a large wooden spoon. *Where does this shit COME from?*

"Sir, what is your emergency?"

Bill takes a deep breath and barks, "Steve Lendowski has been murdered at his home. Fourteen-seventy-six Laurel Mountain

Road. There's also a break-in at twenty-three Meadow Lane—an intruder."

"Sir, calm down. What is your name?"

Fuck that. Bill tosses the cell onto the passenger seat without bothering to disconnect, fires up the WRX, and whips in reverse out of Steve's driveway. A certainty has overcome him, a fact that he knows to be true while having absolutely no real basis for the knowledge: The man with the forked tongue murdered Steve, and right now he is on his way to Bill's home. *Unless, he's already there.*

Bill will remember very little of his frantic drive back to his house. He runs through several stop signs doing sixty-five and bypasses a red light by darting through an EXXON station. Fear rides shotgun, the powerful emotion threatening to loosen his bowels.

Minutes later, Bill accelerates down Meadow Lane to the cul-de-sac and squeals to a halt in front of his house. *Why didn't I think to call Stacey on the cell? Doesn't matter, I'm here.*

Meadow Lane during a late weekday morning is deserted. No Jim Traner in boxers. No cops yet, either. But, there is an entirely out-of-place motorcycle parked on the road two houses down. It's a Harley with big pipes.

Fear negates time and motion. The unusually warm January sun shines as if the world is perfectly sane.

Bill sprints toward his front door, which is closed and intact. He takes no notice of the distant rumble of thunder as he hits the door. It is unlocked. He charges into the house.

The man with the forked-tongue is sitting on a recliner in the living room. He balances Big Billy on one knee and has a large hand wrapped around the toddler's midsection. It takes a second or two for Bill's over-taxed mind to see everything there is to see. When he finally takes it all in, he screams.

The man, who looks so very familiar, holds a child's dismembered leg in his free hand. He raises the leg to his mouth and tears off a hunk of dripping flesh.

Bill's knees buckle. He falls forward to the carpet and barely catches himself with his arms to avoid sprawling flat on his face.

From the demon's knee, Billy makes loud hiccupping sounds. The toddler's eyes are terrible twin circles of shock. The man, who is really a monster, licks blood from the dismembered leg with that amazingly long, forked tongue.

That leg has dark fur on it. Bill's mind comprehends. It's not a child's leg. It's Jeff. The monster, now bouncing Bill's son on his knee and smiling, must have ripped the dog's hind leg from its hip socket. A white bone protrudes from a mass of meat, gristle, and matted fur.

The monster takes another bite out of Jeff's leg, chews lustily, and smacks his lips with pleasure.

From his knees, Bill feels completely helpless. He whimpers, "Please, let my son go."

"Oh, no! We're having too much *fun!*" The monster's voice is resonant and friendly sounding. On some insane level, the tone of the voice almost convinces Bill, in the desperation of hope, that what must surely be a demon from hell actually means no harm.

"Just let him go, please," Bill begs. His lips tingle from too much oxygen. Fearing the answer, Bill whispers, "Where's my wife and daughter?"

"Oh, I think you know."

"Please, please, please," Bill whines.

"Okay, stop that now," says the man-who-is-not-a-man. "You know, she really does have such grand plans for them. You should feel honored."

"Who the hell are you?" Bill is starting to remember that he is a man. Anger rises when he looks at Billy on the monster's knee. The boy is clearly going into shock. Billy's eyes roll back to the whites, and the small body convulses in horrible jerks.

The wind rises in Bill's soul and outside the physical structure of his home. The reversal of emotions inside the father and husband is as quick as flicking a light switch. A moment before, Bill would have crawled on his belly, ate a plate of shit—if only the *fucker* would let go of his son. But, now, anger consumes all. The man, who not thirty minutes before had been overcome with peace and goodwill, is filled with a lust to kill—to tear the throat out of the grinning maniac.

Thunder rumbles outside the house—much closer now.

"Who *am* I?" the monster taunts. "Oh, let's see… Why don't you call me *Gren*."

The monster's eyes capture Bill's full attention for the first time. They are grey and familiar. Bill stares and momentarily forgets his rage.

A slight twitch pulls the flesh at the corner of Gren's left eye. The twitch turns into a wink. The tongue, split in the middle, comes out with deliberate slowness, and licks blood from the bone that protrudes from a piece of the family pet.

Gren smiles.

Bill springs at him from his knees, having formed no intention prior to the act. The leap feels like the slow motion of his dreams.

The recliner goes over backward with Bill's momentum and their combined weight. Billy is flung aside like a doll, and Bill hears his son hit something with a loud *THUMP!*

Somehow, Bill ends up on top. He puts his hands around Gren's neck and squeezes with all of his strength. *It's like trying to strangle a tree trunk.* A fist hits Bill in the middle of the forehead, and another pops him directly on the end of his nose. Blood gushes from his nose and down his throat. Bill's grip loosens. Gren hurls him to the side and leaps on Bill like a cat. A roaring sound fills Bill's ears as two powerful hands clamp down on his throat like a vise.

Stacey, sorry, Bill thinks. He tries to struggle free one last time. Everything is drowned out by the roaring in his ears like a freight train just pulled into the living room. The very last thing Bill remembers is familiar grey eyes inches from his own, and a voice hissing, "I got you now, *FUCKER!*"

Except that Gren doesn't say "fucker"—that's only what Bill's mind allows him to hear. Gren actually says a different two syllable word that begins with the same letter.

When Bill wakes up ten minutes later, his house is gone.

Part III

The Black Moshannon

Ravenous, Tyka prowls the forest, craving the promised feast of human flesh. Her howls, pitiful and lugubrious, echo through the woods.

Warm weather follows the big snow, and the river becomes a raging torrent. The Tunku appears as if from nowhere. Tyka walks forward cautiously and licks her outstretched hand. The Master, who has assumed the form of a young female, assures Tyka that her reward is near.

The next day is unusually warm. Tyka hunkers down in her den and whines. Her ears perk up when a link with some distant, sentient creature is forged. Psychically-endowed knowledge fills her consciousness: Somewhere, a kindred spirit is overcome with fear and pain. The connection breaks.

Perhaps ten miles or so as the crow flies, a dog has come to a violent end.

The sky grows dim. A rumble of thunder heralds the approach of a powerful storm. A great wind rises and roars like a beast. Branches pop like the bones of the small animals Tyka devours.

The violent storm soon passes. Tyka thinks about the connection she felt with the dog—an unforeseen by-product of the gift of consciousness instilled by the Master. For the first time, the wolf experiences a human emotion: empathy.

Thoughts of the dog for which Tyka feels sorry are soon effaced by the desire that has been set within her by the Tunku. Tyka MUST consume human flesh.

⚜ 3:1 ⚜

Bill resumes consciousness, slowly, like waking from an unremembered dream. In this case, the dream is a nightmare.

For a few merciful moments, Bill remains completely disoriented. Cold rain pelts his face. He opens his eyes. A ray of sunshine beams through a rent in the low, grey clouds overhead.

What the fuck?

Bill sits up, winces, and looks around. Tall brown weeds and bracken surround him. He's in the field behind his house. Off to the left, a swath over one hundred yards wide has been cut neatly through the brush and weeds. *Looks like God made one pass through the meadow with a giant vacuum sweeper.*

Bill's eyes follow the swath back toward the cul-de-sac. The landscape looks foreign. Bill is reminded of the scenes he witnessed on the news many times—pictures of communities obliterated by killer tornadoes.

Two houses remain on Meadow Lane, both at the lower end where it meets the main road. Above that, it looks like a bomb detonated. Nothing is recognizable. Where Bill's house once stood is now a tangled waste of debris. The Subaru he'd hastily parked in the street is gone.

As a backdrop to the scene of destruction, a magnificent double rainbow hangs suspended from retreating but sullen storm clouds. Bill remembers his faith in God, and thinks, *Fuck you, asshole.*

The recent past comes together in a landslide that threatens to bury him. Bill gains his feet and stumbles toward the detritus of his life. Intense pain sears through his left knee. He falls and crawls on his hands and knees. Bill is unaware of the frantic chant he emits: "No, No, NO, NOO, *NOOOO!*"

He rises and staggers into the remains of the house. Here is the dishwasher where the living room couch once sat. A tangle of exposed pipes spouts water in a little fountain. Splintered wood and drywall is strewn everywhere.

A family portrait perches unmarred atop a two-by-four: Stacey and Bill beam contented eight-by-eleven pre-Jenna smiles; Krista and Billy look angelic; Jeff, who will become food for a monster, poses and smiles as only black labs can.

Bill cackles like a madman. The world is too bright—too *real*. His mind wants to retreat from this hateful reality.

"Stacey! Krista! Billy! Staceeeeey!"

Bill turns about in aimless circles. Sun shines on his face and illumines a gaping hole at his feet. Down below in the basement lies the remnants of the big screen television—and Billy.

BILLY! A horrible second later Bill perceives that it's not his son, but his son's teddy bear that he sees. The toy is misshapen and sodden with rain.

Light streaks through Bill's mind like rays from above. *He must be in the basement. It's the only way he could have survived.*

Filled with panic-tinged hope, Bill prepares to slide down a ceiling joist into the basement. A voice shouts, "Don't!" Strong hands clutch Bill's shoulder. Everything is a blur. Bill struggles to get free. He grapples with three men who wrestle him out to the street.

"My son!" Bill protests.

"We'll get him!" a volunteer fireman shouts in his face.

Bill stops struggling. His knee is on fire, and sharp pain stabs at his lower back. Bill sinks to the macadam and begins to cry.

The bright sunshine fills with dark spots. The world goes dark.

When he regains consciousness, Bill is strapped to a stretcher. Two men lift the stretcher and put him in the back of an ambulance. One of the guys asks, "Is there anyone else in the house besides your son?"

"I don't know," Bill whispers.

Just before they close the back doors of the ambulance, Bill gets a glimpse of where Jim Traner's house once stood. In Jim's back yard, Bill's Subaru is perched twenty feet off the ground in the mangled limbs of a hundred year old poplar.

When the doors close, Bill slides down a dark tunnel and forgets—if only for a little while.

<h1>⊰ 3:2 ⊱</h1>

Bill wakes in a hospital bed. When he tries to sit up, sharp pain shoots through his lower back. The window to the outside world is a rectangle of undifferentiated black.

How long was I out?

An old man with grey whiskers moans softly in the bed to Bill's left. In the hall, florescent lights shine on buffed linoleum tile. A slight noise, a mere rumor of low-pitched conversation, emanates from an unseen nurse's station down the corridor.

A tear streaks Bill's face. *He's dead. Billy's dead. There's no way he could have survived.* The ache is deep and primal, and beneath—a void that will not be filled. Bill despises the idea that he will continue to exist without his son. He imagines crawling into a hole in the ground, curling into a ball, and waiting to die. Great sobs wrack his body.

He weeps for some unknown time before a new thought—a spark of hope—gives him reason to go on. The beast, Gren, said that Stacey and Krista were still alive. *Maybe he was telling the truth. Maybe they weren't in the house at all.*

With a flicker of hope comes a new emotion.

Bill was always laid back, never understanding the men he saw who stored up every insult and walked around in a perpetual state of rage. On a continuum with road rage maniacs and petty wife beaters at one end, Bill had always been firmly ensconced on the opposite pole. And, so, the seething rage that rises from his gut to fill his chest surprises him.

Laying helpless and in pain, Bill has a vivid fantasy where his hands are around Jenna's delicate throat. He squeezes with all of his strength as she chokes. Her face goes from red to purple. Bill revels in the violence. Finally, he is revolted at what his mind conjures: After he strangles her, Bill pisses on Jenna's lifeless, upturned face.

In less than a single day of his life, Bill has learned the true meaning of both fear and hate.

One thought alone provides a glimmer of hope. Whatever Jenna and her monstrous boyfriend are up to, Bill intuits that murders are not part of the plan.

The light of a new day reveals a uniformed Pennsylvania State Trooper and a plainclothes county detective on either side of Bill's hospital bed. The old man is gone, his bed neatly made up.

"I'm Detective Cook, this is Trooper Belson. Are you William Miller of twenty-three Meadow Lane?"

The plainclothes detective is taking the lead. He is about a head shorter than the trooper, who looks young enough to have graduated from high school a couple of years ago.

"Yes, I am," Bill replies. "And I can give you a description, and the names, of the people who murdered Steve Lendowski and kidnapped my wife and daughter."

Incoherent thought vanishes. Bill tells the police everything, including his affair with Jenna. He is not at all concerned with how bad this makes him look.

The interview lasts over an hour. Bill becomes frustrated at the length of the process. The meticulous questioning of the county detective is frustratingly repetitive. He can't be sure, but the cops seem skeptical, even suspicious.

When the police finally leave, the shock of losing his son hits Bill all over again. His fingers tingle and he has difficulty catching his breath. *Feels like someone hollowed out my guts with an ice cream scoop.* The thought makes Bill think of Steve, and he almost vomits.

Rage. Tears. Fear. Overwhelming sadness. Exhaustion beyond anything Bill has ever felt. For only the second time since he saw Steve's shattered front door, Bill thinks of his renewed piety and the sense of peace he felt just prior to the whirlwind. In response to this unwelcome thought, Bill repeats his sentiment upon waking in the field: "Fuck you, God."

Pain medication knocks him out. He wakes to the local news on the twenty-six-inch Sony television bolted to the wall. A nurse walks in, heavy-set but pretty, excited and apparently overjoyed. Bill is annoyed. He can't focus on her words, and is offended that anyone in the world could be happy when his son is dead.

The nurse turns on CNN. Some weather gal demonstrates the mechanics of an unusually strong cold front that slammed into Gulf of Mexico moisture and created the abnormal January EF5 tornado that devastated Glenville. The program cuts to a taped interview of a female reporter in front of a ruined house, where an old woman—Mrs. Dempsey three houses down from Bill—sobs and waves her arms. The scene shifts to an aerial view, presumably taken from a news helicopter. At first, the picture looks entirely alien to Bill—but, then, he sees it, Meadow Lane, shattered and looking like Godzilla came through after the Apocalypse.

"Wow, that's awesome, who gives a shit," Bill says, not in the least interested in being polite to the nurse. Then, his jaw drops, and he gapes in astonishment.

On the TV, a Pennsylvania State Trooper holds Billy. The boy is a mess but cries with enthusiasm. The toddler is covered with mud and has a bloody scratch above his left eye. An egg-sized bump stands out in the middle of his forehead.

The picture shifts back to the lady reporter, who asks the state trooper a question. Bill doesn't hear what they say.

The nurse can't contain herself any longer. "It's a miracle," she gushes. "They found him three hundred yards from your house, fifty feet up an oak tree! He's here, upstairs in pediatrics!"

The wind that began blowing a hundred years ago on the drive over to Steve's overtakes Bill and becomes a tornado in his mind. He becomes as feeble and limp as a wet dishtowel.

Desperate, close to panic, Bill must see his boy, now, and no amount of pain or hospital personnel will stop him. The nurse is compliant. She helps him into a wheelchair and carts him down a hall and into an elevator. A clean-shaven doctor Bill will not remember joins them on the third floor. He tells him that his son has a concussion and mild hypothermia, but is in stable condition.

The doctor and the nurse continue to talk, excitedly. Bill is unable to focus on the conversation. The word "miracle" is repeated several times. In another minute, he's in a cheerily lit hospital room wall-papered with Sesame Street characters, and lying on a bed is his son—his Billy.

The boy sleeps peacefully. The needle in his arm looks huge. Bill takes in his face—the plump cheeks and pouty little lips, the nasty bruise on his forehead, and the scratch above the eyebrow that will leave a small white scar.

Bill's heart breaks. He falls out of the wheelchair to his knees beside the bed. Hot, salty tears fall on Billy's little hand.

The man, once proud and strong, is meek and awe-struck. Bill is humble, contrite, and grateful to the "Almighty," who is surely watching over them. Kneeling on the cold tile, the hands of the doctor and nurse on his shoulders, the feeling he'd first experienced on the drive over to Steve's is renewed: It's like he's wrapped in a warm cocoon, or womb, where a loving father understands Bill's failings, forgives him, and loves him all the more.

The moment is sublime, and Bill feels with absolute confidence that Stacey and Krista are alive.

Bill silently vows to never doubt God again.

On the way back down in the elevator, a new seed germinates in Bill's mind. Doubt in a loving god does not yet return to gnaw at him, but hope and reverence are displaced by thoughts of Jenna and Gren—and what he's going to do to them.

Bill thinks about Billy lying in a hospital room above his head. The boy's bruised and angelic face provides momentary peace, but this image is followed by a vision of the terrified child sitting on the knee of a stranger, who bounces him playfully as he licks blood from the haunches of the family dog.

Back in bed, as he drifts toward an oxycontin-induced slumber, Bill has two distinct thoughts.

Thank-you, God.

I'm going to kill them.

⊰ 3:3 ⊱

Detective Cook and Trooper Belson return later that day. Acting on Bill's information, the police searched Jenna's dorm room and found the mutilated body of a campus security guard.

Goddamn. Who the hell was I sleeping with?

They go over a lot of the same information. Bill remains patient and composed—willing to do anything to help. The cops want to know more about the man with the forked tongue, who they've been unable to identify.

Bill remembers a new piece of information.

"He said I could call him Gren."

After asking more of the same questions, Cook and Belson leave.

The hospital room is quiet. No roommate. Bill reflects on everything that has happened. The situation is incredible—surreal. Bill is overcome by the strangely comforting notion that neither he nor the police are in control—that events are being *directed*.

A doctor Bill hasn't seen before enters and tells him that his nose is broken, muscles in his lower back are strained, and there is a partial tear in his left anterior cruciate ligament. Bill and his son will likely be released the following day.

Issy stops in, haggard and frantic—no comfort from that source, nor can Bill provide any. After an eternity, Bill's mother-in-law departs for the pediatric department.

Unable to do anything else, Bill watches television. The local news devotes most of its evening telecast to the previous day's freak storm. Aerial footage clearly shows the path of destruction as the twister mowed a channel through the outskirts of the small college town of Glenville. The tornado bypassed the campus entirely, demolished a silo and barn at the Eldridge pig farm, and bulldozed through the woods to the south of Bill's development before erasing much of the Meadow Lane cul-de-sac.

The newscast returns live to the studio, and Veronica Wayne reports three people on Meadow Lane were killed, including Jim Traner. Bill thinks, *If God did send a tornado to rescue me and Billy, He was a trifle sloppy.*

He sits up straight when Stacey and Krista appear on the TV—pictures of them from his wallet that he gave to Trooper Belson.

"Investigators have declined to give us additional details," the anchor says, "but they believe the mother and daughter may be the victims of a kidnapping. Anyone with information should contact the state police at the number posted on your screen.

"In what police fear may be a related crime, the body of a Glenville University professor was discovered not far from the campus. Steve Lendowski, a fifty-five year old English professor, was found deceased yesterday in his home. Kevin Donnely reports to us from the scene."

The newscast goes live to a reporter standing alone in front of Steve's ranch house. Yellow police tape surrounds the property. Bill shivers when he sees that the shattered door has been boarded over with plywood.

Back in the studio, Veronica hands it off to her co-anchor, Larry Thomas. "Yes, indeed, Veronica, things have taken an unsettling turn in the sleepy college town of Glenville. Authorities now tell us that yet another body has been discovered. A Glenville University security officer was found deceased in a campus dorm room just this morning. Police suspect foul play, but won't speculate as to whether the campus incident is related to the Lewdowski killing. Hillary Tennesson has a live report from the Glenville campus."

The newscast shifts to the twenty-something Hillary, who interviews Detective Cook in front of Old Main. Cook merely repeats information the news anchors already provided, but then adds, "We have several persons of interest we'd like to interview."

On the screen, the live interview is replaced by a picture of Jenna—probably her campus photo ID—followed by an artist's rendering of Bill!

No, that's not me. It's a sketch of Gren based on my description to the police. Damn, I didn't realize how much we look alike!

The program turns to Tina Carmichael with the weather. "Back to reality, folks," Tina says with a sparkling smile. "It's going to feel a lot more like January, with three to six inches of snow in the forecast."

Bill dozes off. When he wakes, it's dark outside. *Those pain meds are some good shit.*

The hospital is very quiet—no sound from the hall, and someone turned off the television. A strong wind howls around the brick facade of the building. Bill looks to his left and discovers that sometime during his lengthy nap a new roommate arrived. He can't make out the guy's features in the darkened room, but he sure could hear him snoring.

Man, the new guy sounds like he's running a saw mill over there.

Bill is amused, but he becomes alarmed when the snores transition to a series of gasps and hiccups.

"Hey, buddy, maybe you should roll over," Bill says. His suggestion elicits more snores that almost sound like muffled, choking laughter.

"Hey, Mister," Bill says, loud enough to wake him.

The man stops snoring and rolls over to face Bill across five feet of hospital room. It's Gren, who opens his mouth wide. The forked tongue flicks out, and keeps coming, until it wavers through the air between the beds like a charmed cobra. Wet flesh caresses Bill's face.

Bill wakes to his darkened hospital room. A demon does not occupy the adjacent bed. Bill yells nonetheless—twice. An older nurse comes running in.

"You must think I'm crazy." Bill is embarrassed and apologetic, but the nurse is a sweetheart. She wipes the sweat from his brow and reassures him like a mother hen.

When Bill sleeps again, a new nightmare greets him.

He plays chess with Steve in the dead man's den. Steve is winning as usual, and let's Bill know it.

The scene shifts to Steve's kitchen. The two men sit across from each other at the small circular table.

Steve says, "I'm dead, Bill." He rises and holds onto his midsection with both hands. Blood pours through Steve's fingers in rivers. He takes a labored step around the table. Intestines spill out onto the linoleum with a loud *SPLAT!* As he shuffles toward Bill, his guts leave a bloody snail's trail behind him.

"She wants you to go to the Black Moshannon," Steve rasps. Blood bubbles out of his mouth. "You better hurry."

Bill's eyes pop open, and there is no interim between sleep and waking—no disorientation. He doesn't scream this time.

That one was in High-Def.

The hospital room is dark. The wind whispers some secret beyond the black rectangle of window. Bill rises from the bed. The pain is not as bad. He looks in the closet, and finds a plastic bag containing the shoes, muddy jeans, dress shirt, and sport coat he was wearing the day his life was turned upside down.

Time to go.

⚜ 3:4 ⚜

Bill strides down the shoulder of a deserted, two-lane rural route. It's the middle of the night, and January has returned. Chilly plumes of wind-driven cloud speed across the waning moon. He's a mile outside of town and headed for the Black Moshannon Forest, some ten miles distant.

A merciless gust sucks the air from Bill's lungs. The muddy clothes he retrieved from the closet provide little protection. *Better than walking down the road in a hospital gown with my ass hanging out.*

Bill trudges on, the pain in his leg and back growing with each step. The pain meds stopped working long ago. Bill stops in mid-stride—not from the pain, but with what he thinks is a flash of clarity.

What the fuck am I doing?

The cold and pain prevented sustained reflection on any one subject since he began his midnight jaunt, but now, the brutal reality of his immediate circumstances cause Bill to soberly consider the choice he's made. *Am I really going to hike ten miles to a forest in the middle of the night because of a dream?*

An internal debate ensues. The assistant professor of sociology argues for reason and scoffs at notions like prescient dreams, Noah and his ark, and freak January tornadoes that save fathers and sons.

At the other pole of Bill's thought is unmitigated belief. In this place, Bill is released from the limitations of human reason: the supernatural is real and the possibility of God becomes more than possibility.

In this latter place, hope produces a species of joy—the assurance that things are working out as they should. Here, the King James Version of the Bible suggests literal truth, and spiritual conflict among angels and fallen angels is a tangible reality in the dark, bitter night.

A layer of cloud covers the moon. The first feather of snow brushes his cheek. The wind makes brown stalks of corn on either side of the road whisper in some unknown, sibilant tongue. Bill glances nervously over his shoulder back in the direction of town. Comfort from belief in a loving God is mitigated by the idea's antithesis: *If God exists, then why not The Devil? And, if there is a Devil, did I just screw one of his concubines?*

I must be losing my mind.

Standing indecisive on the deserted road shoulder, rational explanations for the recent events flood Bill's mind. He recalls a clip on *The World's Most Amazing Videos* where a child Billy's age was rescued from a tree after a tornado destroyed his home—the present "miracle" wasn't even unique.

Unusual shit happens all the time. It's not supernatural, it's coincidence. Sure, that was weird how the tornado hit when it did—just at the right moment. But, that sure as hell doesn't mean God rescued us. Jenna and Gren aren't monsters that can manipulate my dreams—they're just a couple of crazy assholes. The world's loaded with them.

"Fuck this."

Bill turns and starts walking back to the hospital.

Flakes of snow tickle his face. He can't feel the pain in his ears or cheeks anymore, because they are numb. Bill laughs without mirth when he realizes the great mysteries of the cosmos are irrelevant when the potential for death by freezing arises.

Wish I had my cell.

A tickle at the back of his mind makes Bill hesitate. He slows his pace. The implication of rejecting faith in God rears up and frightens Bill more than any deranged lunatic ever could.

He stops and glances over his shoulder in the direction of the distant forest.

What type am I?

He falls to his knees on the road shoulder. Loose gravel gouges his kneecaps through his jeans. He barely notices the pain.

Raising his face to the sky, Bill shouts, "Okay, then, how about a fucking *SIGN!*"

Headlights appear in the road ahead. The vehicle is coming from the town, headed toward the forest. The lights illumine a swirling mass of snowflakes. A truck comes into view.

Coincidence—hell, it IS a road.

The rig slows and comes to a stop about twenty yards past Bill.

Oh, what the hell.

Bill turns around and walks up to the driver's side of the idling truck. The window is down.

"Hey, buddy, you don't have a gun do you?" The driver, a young man in his early twenties, wears a heavy brown coat and a Pittsburgh Penguins cap. "You didn't seem to be going my way, but I can do a quick run back to town so you don't freeze your butt off."

"No, no gun," Bill says. "I think I might be losing my marbles, but other than that, I'm perfectly harmless."

"Hop in," the driver replies, and Bill climbs aboard.

The rig, hauling a load of fresh cut timber, has a warm and friendly cab. A picture of a pretty, young brunette, all of eighteen, is pasted above the heating vent on the panel. For a minute, Bill simply enjoys the warmth and physical comfort emanating from the vents.

Aware that the young man is looking at him as much as the road ahead, Bill finally says, "Thanks a lot, pal, I think you saved my life."

"No problem, mister. I couldn't call myself much of a Christian if I didn't stop to pick up a fella' on a night like this. I'll turn us around the first chance I get. Did your car break down or something?"

"Actually, I'm going your way," Bill says. "It's kinda' hard to explain, but I have business in the Black Moshannon Forest."

Bill is surprised at his own certainty and the expeditious swing of his mood and thoughts. *Am I a true believer again? I should make up my freakin' mind!*

"Well, it does sound a little crazy," the trucker says. "But then again, who am I to judge?

"I'm going right through there, up over the Laurel Ridge. I start early to get my load over to the mill at Farmingdale. I don't mind, though, because I get to spend evenings with my sweetie, Julie. You see her there on the dash? Man, I'm the luckiest guy in the world. We're expecting a baby in the spring. I shouldn't call it luck though—more like a blessing, you know what I mean?"

Bill doesn't answer. He examines the young man with black whiskers and the provincial Penguins cap. *Angels and demons,* Bill thinks with a shake of his head. He follows that thought with one that suggests the angels have won a round.

"I think maybe I do know what you mean," Bill says. "So, do you have a name picked out yet?"

"Yep. My name's Will, but my little man will be Steve—after Saint Stephen. You know, the first martyr."

"No kidding."

"You betcha'."

Some minutes pass in comfortable silence.

Bill says, "I'm blessed too, but sometimes I forget."

"Oh, Dude, not good. That's the path to the dark side, young Padawan. Julie and me, we're in it forever."

Bill gets the *Star Wars* reference, and can't help but feel that the warm cab and the dark night of Western Pennsylvania rushing by outside the passenger window are starkly surreal.

The men don't speak further for some minutes, since everything that needed saying has been said. Every now and again, a gust of wind rocks the truck. The snow swirls thickly outside.

Will reduces gear and begins to climb the Laurel Ridge. The only sound is the soothing grumble of the rig's engine as it labors up the grade.

The truck slows to fifteen miles per hour as the incline steepens. The trees of the Black Moshannon envelop either side of the road. The darkness between the boles is lightened by accumulating snow.

Bill is close to nodding off when an apparition appears on the shoulder of the road—a wisp of a young woman cloaked in fresh snowfall. Bill looks intently in the side mirror, fully awake but disoriented.

"Did you see that?" Bill asks.

"See what?"

"That woman! She was standing right on the shoulder, on my side!"

"No, I didn't see anyone," Will says. "Then again, a woman on the side of the road at three a.m. in the Black Moshannon is about par for the course tonight, isn't it?" He pulls over to the slushy shoulder.

"I guess you'll be getting out here."

Bill answers in the affirmative.

As he swings out of the cab, Will says, "Hey, wait a minute." He removes his thick jacket and rummages beside the seat. "Here you go." Bill catches the jacket and a Pittsburgh Steelers tassel hat. They make eye contact, and Bill knows it isn't necessary to voice his thank-you.

"Do you want me to call the cops or something?" Will asks.

"Don't bother. I think I'm on my own. Thanks very much, Samaritan."

"You got it, pardner. But I don't think you're on your own."

Will waves and pulls off. When the lights from the truck disappear around a curve in the road, Bill feels lonelier than he has in his entire life.

I'm standing on the side of the road, in the middle of the night, near the summit of the Laurel Ridge, in the midst of a Western Pennsylvania snowstorm. Yep. I'm doing the right thing.

Snow falls in wet, heavy sheets. Bill is thankful for Will's gifts.

He searches the roadside, back and forth over the same area three times. No footprints. *Maybe the snow covered them already.*

Not at all surprised by another enigma, Bill enters the woods close to the place where he saw the feminine "apparition."

The wind slackens. Snow comes straight down to form a white veil over the world. Several inches have already accumulated. The white blanket and the mostly full moon behind the clouds give Bill plenty of light to navigate through the trees.

Now that the wind has died, there is a deep silence in the midst of the forest, broken only by the whisper of snowflakes brushing against the green laurel. For some time, Bill sees nothing but the trees, the falling snow, and a mature stand of mountain laurel that blocks any view of the terrain ahead.

Gravity and the lay of the land naturally lead Bill sideways across the ridge and steadily downhill. After fifteen minutes of trudging, a deep ravine opens up at his feet.

Bill hears something in the deep cleft—maybe a distant voice. The sound is so low that he thinks it may be a trick of his mind.

There it is again! Sounds like a child!

Bill slides down the ravine on his backside because there is no other way without breaking his neck. Some forty feet down, he reaches the rock-strewn bottom, through which flows a small mountain stream. The gurgle of the run sounds something like a distant voice. Bill questions his perception of the world.

A branch snaps. So quiet and still is the forest in its shroud of snow that Bill cannot talk himself into believing it was imaginary.

The subtle *snick* of another breaking twig comes from the lip of the ravine. Bill doesn't believe it's a deer moving through the woods.

Something is stalking me.

He moves down the ravine and tries to steer clear of the running water. The gurgle of storm run-off can't quite block the sound of snapping branches above and on either side.

"Help!"

A child's voice—no doubt about it.

Glancing nervously up one side of the ravine, Bill sees the distinct outline of a humanoid shape pass between two trees at the rim of the gully.

"Daddy!"—faint but unmistakable.

It's Krista; Bill is sure of it. He rushes down the incline, reckless and unconcerned with treacherous rocks and stalking phantoms.

Bill shouts, "KRISTA," and trips over a root. Pain explodes in his shin where it strikes a rock. Bill ignores the pain and splashes down the creek bed in the direction of the voice.

The darkness ahead lightens. A chasm looms. Bill's momentum carries him forward. He hurtles through snow-filled air in what seems like slow motion—two seconds of free-fall perceived as minutes, like the dreamy quality of the time before an out-of-control automobile makes impact.

The unreal perception of timeless flight is interrupted by a plunge into cold, deep water. Bill has stumbled off a twelve-foot cliff into the storm-swollen waters of the Little Kittanning River. He misses a submerged boulder by inches.

All is darkness and swirling bubbles. Bill breaks the surface, but he cannot pull air into his lungs—the deep chill of the water constricts his chest.

The class IV rapid sweeps Bill over a six foot ledge. Just as he's coming up, the river carries him over another ledge. Submerged in cold, swirling chaos, Bill thinks, *This might be it.*

Just when he knows he must suck in the freezing river water, Bill breaks the surface. He gasps and manages to sip tiny gulps of frosty air. Small waves slap him in the face and choke him. Finally, the river flattens out. Bill rolls onto his back.

Kicking feebly, he manages to reach the boulder-strewn shore. He coughs out water and collapses on a rock with his feet still in the stream.

Unable to feel relief or appreciate the fact that he has escaped death, Bill lays on the rocky shore like a dead thing. Although he can breathe a little easier now that he's out of the freezing water, his muscles are still constricted. Pain fills his consciousness as completely as the pleasure he felt when climaxing with Jenna.

After a few minutes of agony, Bill slowly raises his head. The snow has stopped, and the moon is bright enough for Bill to make out the little waterfall he plunged over about seventy-five yards up the raging river. Amidst the foaming rapids is a truck-sized boulder, and just above that, Bill sees a sight so strange he gapes and blinks like an owl.

A person is standing in the middle of the river—on top of the water.

That ain't Jesus, Bill thinks, and giggles hysterically. He blinks and rubs his eyes like a child. The figure—a woman—glides across the water above the rapid. There is something else, a mass of shadowy material rising several feet around and above her head and shoulders.

Bill feels someone looking at him.

He's behind me.

An incredibly strong hand grabs Bill by the collar of the truck driver's coat and jerks him to his feet like a rag doll.

"Now, where were we?" a familiar voice queries.

It's Gren. He jerks Bill's two hundred pound body around like a child in line for a good spanking.

Son-of-a-bitch looks like he grew six inches!

Gren grips Bill by the throat with one hand. Bill's feet leave the ground. He shakes Bill like a terrier with a rat. Gren raises his free hand—about the size of a garden spade—and slaps Bill across the face. The sound of the blow is short and sharp, like the report of a small caliber rifle.

The explosive pain in the side of Bill's face is momentary. The freezing cold, pain, and cares of this world recede.

As darkness descends, Bill thinks: *I blew it.*

⊰ 3:5 ⊱

Bill is back in Steve Lendowski's den. The dream is almost like a memory that recalls a conversation the two of them had in the week before Stacey said it was time to come home. The heavy drinking was behind him, and Bill's mood at that time was elevated by his rediscovered faith.

In the realm of delirium, this is how Bill remembers the conversation with his soon-to-be-murdered friend:

Steve is kicked back on a black leather couch smoking a joint, while Bill sits in a recliner with a Rolling Rock.

"So, you're not going to start handling snakes and speaking in tongues, are you?" Steve asks with a smirk. The topic is Bill's recent conversion. Steve, a secular Jew, is too good a friend to genuinely mock, but is not above stirring the pot to get a good argument started.

"So what if I do?" Bill replies with a smile. "Do you suppose the creator of the universe is incapable of endowing his servants with minor supernatural powers?"

"Look, I'm just saying, Billy, you're an educated guy. Hell, science told us some time ago that a man can't live inside a whale's gut!"

"Science!" Bill scoffs. His fire is stoked. He's fully prepared and willing to argue the incredible—even if he still maintains his own private doubts.

"How often do scientists get it wrong, Steve? How many times have really brilliant physicists twisted themselves into knots because a new discovery didn't comport with their standard cosmological models?

"Remember that crowd a couple years ago that thought they discovered neutrinos travel faster than the speed of light? Turned out there was a loose wire or somebody tripped over a power cord.

"I won't apologize for having a broad enough mind to recognize that some extremely powerful entity, beyond man's ability to comprehend, is responsible for the miracle of the universe."

Bill stops when he realizes he's been preaching—probably came across as frenetic and overzealous.

Steve is kicked back, glassy-eyed and amused. He beckons Bill to proceed with a motion of his hand.

Bill tones it down a notch. "Look man, I know you don't think I'm some blind zealot. But, Steve, you remind me of all these pretentious academics who put on airs as if they are *sooo* very thoughtful. The truth is they merely box themselves in with ideologies. Or else, they worship at the altar of science. You can't be that narrow-minded, my friend."

"Sure, man," Steve replies. He is clearly very high. "One time I took enough acid to believe I could levitate the student union building. Opiate of the masses, baby, go for it!"

Bill glares at Steve and crosses his arms.

"Okay, so you don't believe in miracles. Fine. The stick bug that looks like a stick got that way by accident over the course of evolutionary deep time, and the terminal patient who defies the doctor and lives another thirty years—well, that's just one of those things. All of existence is just one, big chaotic accident, right?"

Even stoned, Steve senses Bill's anger. He tries to get serious. "I know you're sincere, Bill. It's just… I don't see it. The shit, the grime of this world, the pain—that's real. People die in agony. There is no justice.

"In your religion, a man who does *evil* his whole life, but converts on his deathbed, is 'saved.' But, a person who does *good* his entire life burns in Hell because he fails to acknowledge your particular deity! If that's how God works, then he must be pretty fucked up."

Bill shrugs, his anger spent. "I just wish you could acknowledge the *possibility* that it's true. Some pretty bright people have reasoned their way to a belief in God, you know."

"But they haven't reasoned their way to a literal interpretation of the Bible," Steve retorts. "Transubstantiation, the parting of the Red Sea, the belief that Jesus Christ is the son of God—no amount of reason can get you there, man."

"No, that's called faith," Bill says in a low voice.

"Well, I'm glad you got faith in something, brotha.' Me, I'll stick to the 'herb.'"

Steve inhales deeply, trying to end the argument with some levity. But, he can't resist a final thrust. "I'm just saying, if I's God, and had the power to make things right, I'd wave my 'magic wand' or some shit and make it happen.

"Think about it. Just how *does* a supremely good and all-powerful entity tolerate the depravity of this world?"

Bill doesn't need to search for an answer to this common argument. He replies, "Since you don't believe in God, I'm not surprised you don't give the Devil his due, Steve. God gave us free will—so don't blame him for mankind's vile behavior.

"People are all screwed up, fallible and lost—even someone who 'does good' his entire life. Christians are no different, Steve. We just choose to believe there's a God who wants to forgive us."

The discussion ends with an awkward silence. In his dream-memory, grief and pity overcome Bill. He remembers that Steve set him on the path to prayer and faith in the first place.

Now, in the midst of delirium, Bill's mind manufactures a more suitable ending to the argument—one that he thinks might even have put the tiniest crack in Steve Lendowski's secular armor.

Tossing and turning on a dank, smelly couch, semi-conscious and fever-stricken, Bill mutters, "You don't have any hope, Steve. It's about *hope*."

⚔ 3:6 ⚔

One time in college, Bill gave plasma for extra cash and passed out. Slowly waking from that experience was a lot like his present state, where consciousness is regained as if emerging from the water of a deep lake. In the beginning, there are voices like the adults in Charlie Brown cartoons: "*Wah – wah – wuh – wa – wuh – wah – wuh*"—incomprehensible and devoid of meaning.

A voice becomes briefly clearer: *Wa – wuh – il – live, lucky for you*," but it soon dissolves into more nonsense syllables. Bill descends back into darkness.

He's swimming for his life, trying to regain the surface of a raging whitewater. In this dream, there is no sensation of numbing cold, and the brush of bubbles against his cheeks is only imagined. At times, the rapids emit a low steady hum—like a small motor.

Bill's first waking vision is of weak daylight filtering through a dirty windowpane. Ice on the outside of the glass makes the view more translucent than transparent, but he can see the bare twigs of a tree against a leaden, January sky.

Swimming out of another disturbing dream he can't remember, Bill seems to wake. He fixes his gaze on a roaring fireplace. Mesmerized by the orange-red hues of the shifting embers, Bill stares at the fire for hours. A low hum periodically intrudes into his fevered reality—almost like the choppy drone of an engine.

He becomes aware of an old woman sitting in a chair not far from the fireplace. She is very old and wrinkled, but kind-looking with a blue shawl draped across her shoulders.

When Bill wakes the next time, the woman is bending over him. He gets a good look at her face. She is older than he thought—must surely be in her nineties. Bill's attention shifts from the sagging flesh of the woman's neck and the leathery appearance of her skin to bright blue eyes, comforting and young-looking with whites unblemished.

A most distinguishing feature on this face is a large mole sprouting two thick, black hairs, placed indelicately low on the woman's left cheek.

Might have been a beauty mark back sometime before the invention of the internal combustion engine, Bill thinks. He resists the urge to cackle like a lunatic.

The old woman gently spoons some hot broth into him. The simple effort of propping himself on his elbows to receive the thin soup exhausts Bill. He collapses back into uneasy sleep.

Time does not exist. Bill's consciousness is clouded by fever, and delirium makes waking like dreaming. He can't be sure what is real.

Tiny snowflakes come to rest on the ledge outside the dirty window. Bill sees individual grains of snow in all of their infinitely complex shapes as they settle. *If this is a dream, it's the most realistic one I've ever had.*

Bill hears voices in the room. He turns and sees that the old woman has been joined by a companion—an octogenarian in a red flannel shirt, suspenders, and grey trousers. They sit whispering at a small table not far from the glowing fire.

Bill examines his surroundings more fully. He appears to be in a small cabin. The floor is of aged wood, unvarnished but solid. The walls are paneled in knotty pine. The mountain stone fireplace takes up one end of the room.

A slight draft from directly behind his head must indicate the location of the only door to the outside. In the wall opposite the fireplace, a closed door probably leads to a bedroom and privy. Directly across from the couch where Bill lays is a small sink. Above the sink, cups, pots, and various cooking implements hang from hooks in the darkly stained tongue-and-groove ceiling.

The only furnishings are the couch, a rocker by the fire, and the little table where the couple sips what smells like green tea. A drab, six by eight foot rug covers a section of the wooden floor. Bill doesn't see the outlines of a trapdoor beneath the rug.

He looks more closely at the elderly couple. They glance at him in a kindly fashion.

They must have saved my life. But how? Gren could flick them aside like flies.

He tries to speak. The old man and woman seem to withdraw down a long corridor—an effect of the high fever, which still threatens Bill's life.

Just before slipping back into dark and troubled dreams, Bill imagines that the old gent gives him a look with grey eyes that are no longer kindly. The man gives him a malevolent wink. No, it's just a twitch in the flesh below the left eye.

Bill thinks that if he somehow lives another forty years, he might end up resembling the old man.

He wakes to find the elderly woman fumbling with his pants. He's revolted, but instantly ashamed when he realizes she is only helping him with a makeshift bedpan. Bill is too sick and helpless to feel humiliation.

A new nightmare torments Bill. The woman is at his pants again. She takes him in her hand, and he quickly becomes erect. He wants to refuse her but cannot speak. She straddles him. Wrinkled breasts dangle and flop as the woman grinds into him with rapid thrusts of her hips. Bill ejaculates with a hideous merger of pleasure and revulsion. The crone cackles obscenely.

Bile and broth burn his throat as he vomits. The old woman appears with a towel. She is fully clothed and looks at him kindly with beautiful, blue eyes. Her mole doesn't seem as prominent, and the wrinkles in her skin appear less deep. She gently wipes sour vomit from the corner of Bill's mouth.

I'm very ill. My mind is playing tricks. How else could she look like she's thirty years younger?

The pattern continues, waking and dreaming fused into a nightmare reality. Large passages of time involve Bill staring blankly out the window at gently falling precipitation. The swirling snow materializes into looming shapes of disfigured woodland creatures. An ephemeral snow bear grins in the window at him. When he closes his eyes, the flakes fall in endless curtains of black dots behind his lids.

The next time Bill wakes, the fire has burned low. There is

just enough light to reveal a horror show unfolding on the little table. Bill's attendants, no longer so aged, are engaged in vigorous intercourse. The man's suspenders dangle in a heap around his ankles as he thrusts inside an attractive blonde bent over the table. He rams into her so hard she must grip the edges of the table with her hands to avoid a tumble.

Bill looks more closely at the woman. A small beauty mark has replaced the grotesque mole on her left cheek. Bill looks at the man again. He thrusts like a jackhammer. The muscles in his neck bulge as he approaches climax. But, it's no longer a human neck—it's covered with dark, thick fur.

Bill yells.

The "old man" has the long, narrow head of a giant weasel. The dying fire casts just enough light for Bill to see a twitch in the flesh below a beady, grey eye.

The final horror before the return of stark, lucid consciousness is an explosive sex act in a completely dark room. A young woman is on top of Bill, grinding and thrusting. Her skin is smooth and supple. Bill knows that it's Jenna, but he doesn't care anymore. He becomes a willing participant and cups full, firm breasts with his hands. Pleasure consumes him—negates his identity.

When Bill cries out with his orgasm, sharp nails dig into his chest. A voice he knows intimately whispers, "I can't wait to see how your daughter *fucks*, Professor."

⚜ 3:7 ⚜

Darkness.

Now—full, undistorted reality.

Bill lies on his back on a filthy, mildew-encrusted couch. The charming cabin is actually a dank shack in the woods, pervaded by a deep winter chill. Only dead ashes remain in the fireplace. The red stubs of three spent flares lie on the hearth, evidently used to start the fire.

A deep and profound silence shrouds the cabin. Bill's fever is gone, but his body feels as if it has only halfway recovered from a serious traffic accident. He wonders how many of the recent events actually happened. The last thing he is absolutely certain of is being attacked by Gren at the river.

The cabin is quite cold. Outside, a dim morning shines through the window. Bill rises, winces at the pain in his back and knee, and almost collapses back to the filthy couch. He manages to get on his feet and examine the cabin.

The only bedroom has one furnishing, a darkly stained twin mattress lying in a corner. A tiny bathroom off the bedroom contains a shower stall and a toilet containing a bowlful of unspeakable filth. A used condom lay on the floor. Some poet has scratched, "Kevin loves Kim," into the moldy paneling.

"He must," Bill says, and returns to the main chamber.

In the kitchen sink is grime, dead beetles, and a few dirty pans. Empty packets of Lipton's *Cup O' Soup* are scattered over the counter. Bill's attention shifts to the table where Gren and Jenna copulated so vigorously. *Or was that just a dream?* Bill can't be sure, but gives that particular item no further thought. His attention is captivated by what lays on the table.

Bill picks up the sealed white envelope. *Professor* is written there in a script he recognizes from having read so many of Jenna's unnaturally advanced essays on sociological theory.

Hands shaking, Bill tears open the envelope and reads the letter inside.

Dear Professor,

So, was that fuck last night the best yet, or what? But you know, sweetie, the look on your face when "Granny Jenna" was doing you may have been more gratifying than my orgasm!

You must have so many questions, beginning with "Why?"

The answer is—because! Because I CAN, and because I LIKE it!

If it's any consolation—if you're still troubled by that silliest and most useless human emotion (guilt)—let me assure you that what I get out of all this is far more satisfying when the target is a fundamentally good person.

Seeing you betray your values and principles, and so forth. The cherry on the cake! Yummy!

Wondering about Stacey and Krista? Oh, dear. I'm not sure how to tell you this. Not all of the news is good. Stacey didn't make it, Bill. I guess all of the excitement from getting hammered by someone as large as "Gren" was too much for her. Is that really what he told you to call him? Gren? That's so cute. The clever boy!

But, I digress. May as well put it right out there. GRENDEL (Do you get it yet, Bill?) just about split your wife down the middle he fucked her so hard with that massive cock of his. But, you know, Bill, not meaning to be cruel or anything—I think she kind of liked it there for a while. You must know how she moans down deep when she comes? And pants like a dog? Too sexy!

ANYWAYS... let us turn to the subject of your daughter. What a truly precious child. She doesn't understand yet, but she will—in time. Don't fear for her, Bill. She's mine. With my guidance, she'll become the most talented child whore on the Bangkok market.

What a delicious little harlot Krista will be for all of those European and American tourists to fill with their spunk!

What? Did you think this would have a happy ending? No, Bill. You disappointed me. You broke things off with ME. Before I was DONE WITH YOU.

Naughty boy. You'll have to pay.

I suggest you follow the trail that begins about a hundred yards off the north end of the cabin. Follow it to the end, and just maybe I'll do you a favor, and not make you watch when Gren breaks in your little Krista.

Oh, and, I know you have a Ph.D. and all, but just in case you never read Beowulf, and your skeptical academic mind hasn't managed to process all of the not-so-subtle hints: The charming fellow with the forked tongue is our son.

Big for a four month old, isn't he? Poor baby, he's aging so fast. And, how he hates his DADDY! I hope you feel some measure of gratitude when you realize he would have killed you at the river if it wasn't for me.

Well, better get moving up that path, professor!

J.

As he reads the note, Bill's mind becomes a confused, emotional tangle—too much incredible information to process in too short a time. Toward the end, his free hand clenches into a fist. He nearly passes out before he realizes that he's been hyperventilating.

Bill says, "Bullshit."

Spiritual warfare, God and Satan, and the mysteries of the supernatural are quite distant in the thin winter light that filters into the shack. The world is hyper-real—a stark contrast to Bill's recent existence.

He thinks about prayer, but he can't do it. The idea that an invisible god might save him seems hopelessly silly.

As he begins to search the drawers under the sink for a weapon or anything else that might prove useful, Bill's mind regards the strange events of the previous days. He quickly discards supernatural explanations with a scoff.

Always fickle, Bill is the skeptical, materialist professor again. Questions like, "How is it that a dream leads me to the forest, and there's Jenna?" are easily rebutted with ordinary explanations, such as, "I manufactured the dream and was followed to the forest by Maniac one and Maniac two, who were watching the hospital to see what I would do next."

What can't be explained by fever-induced delirium, tricks of the moon-light, coincidence, and a pair of lunatics? Divinely-inspired tornadoes and a monster that grows from egg in the womb to middle-aged man in four months? Yeah, right, and the Easter Bunny and Santa Claus are going to come on over to the shack so we can have a tea party with crumpets and little sandwiches.

No weapons, not even a fork. Bill gathers up the coat and hat the truck driver gave to him and heads for the door. He's in a hurry. The fever that nearly killed him is already returning.

Bill has no clear conception of what he is doing, or why. *Kill-ing to be done*—he knows that much.

He walks stiff-legged over the moldy rug in the middle of the floor. He doesn't notice the slight give in the wood that might have alerted him to the presence of a trapdoor—if he was lucid.

A piece of broken mirror on the floor by the door catches Bill's eye. He picks it up and takes a look. The face staring back is familiar but gaunt. A large, purplish bruise shows where Grendel slapped him. His nose is no longer straight. His eyes are glassy. He also has about five day's growth of beard stubble on his cheeks.

Accounting for the time in the hospital, Bill figures he's been in the shack for three days.

Bill exits the cabin. The dim light of a cloudy day nearly blinds him. As he stumbles for the trail, Bill is too drained to consider notions of hope, reason, or the realm of the possible.

On the slope above the cabin, a grey wolf watches as a man staggers into the woods.

Tyka leaps forward for the kill.

Part IV

In the Cellar

The one who called her—the powerful demon who sometimes disguises herself as a young blonde woman—has brought Tyka prey at last. First, an adult woman and female child, then an adult male are brought to the cabin. Tyka can smell their blood. The man is to be hers.

Two days pass as Tyka prowls the forest around the cabin. On the third day, the man emerges. Clearly ill and weak, he stumbles up a trail. Tyka springs forward for the kill.

"Halt!" A command invades her consciousness—an order from the Tunku. Tyka must wait yet again.

She whines and follows the man from a distance. The faint smell of a dog emanates from him—the odor of the animal whose violent death Tyka sensed.

Thoughts of the dog trouble Tyka; Jenna's gift of human consciousness has unexpectedly imbued her with the capacity to feel pity.

Tyka stops and slinks into a thick stand of rhododendron. The Tunku's offspring appears. It stalks the man from the opposite side of the path. It looks like a man, but its spirit reminds Tyka of the woodland snakes she avoids. There is a dynamic and unpredictable quality about the man/serpent. For the first time, Tyka experiences real fear.

"You must wait."

The command comes again. The voice is Jenna's, translated inside the mind of the wolf. Tyka obeys—she has no choice— and withdraws deeper into the thick verdure.

The man passes up the trail deeper into the woods. Tyka crouches and watches as the man/serpent follows him at some small distance.

❧ 4:1 ❧

In the days after Bill Miller's disappearance, a dozen police representing various jurisdictions at the local, state, and federal level sift through the debris at the ruined home and interview scores of persons, including neighbors, students, and university personnel. A local cop finds the remains of the family dog in the ruins of the Miller home, so that part of the husband's story checks out—although it doesn't prove a guy with a forked tongue who calls himself "Gren" mutilated the animal.

The tornado dominates the local news in the days after the storm. Billy Miller, Glenville's own "miracle baby," figures prominently in the coverage.

The media buzz becomes frenetic when Bill Miller disappears from the hospital in the middle of the night. The local news channels and all four network affiliates in Pittsburgh run pictures of Bill and Jenna, who are wanted for questioning by police in the disappearance of Stacey and Krista Miller, as well as the murders of a university faculty member and a security guard.

William Hegins, who drives a truck for a local lumber company, does not watch the news on a regular basis—so it is not until the local channel has been showing the photos of Bill and Jenna for three days that he recognizes the guy to whom he'd given a lift.

Drinking his "morning" coffee at five-thirty in the afternoon, Hegins sits contentedly on the couch with his sweetie, Julie, curled up under his right arm. He puts down the coffee at Julie's insistence and feels her stomach, where his unborn child kicks with enthusiasm. That's when the picture of Bill appears on the television.

Five minutes later, Will is on the phone with Chief Richard Prentiss of the Glenville PD.

At first light the next morning, on the day Bill sets out from the cabin at Jenna's instruction, a dozen police search the slopes of the Laurel Ridge—but on the wrong side of the Little Kittanning River.

County Detective Jim Cook is interested in a certain hospital security tape. As police and volunteers search the woods, he watches the tape for the fourth time, his nose inches from the screen. Cook is flanked by two other cops: Richard Prentiss, Glenville's Chief of Police, and Kevin Dreyfus, a field agent from the Pittsburgh office of the FBI.

Cook thinks Richard Prentiss is a straight shooter who says what he thinks, but Dreyfus is clearly a pretentious asshole, called in because of the alleged kidnapping.

"What the hell *is* that?" Prentiss mutters.

"Unknown," replies Dreyfus with a sniff. The field agent paces through the hospital security office and adopts an authoritative tone.

"Let's go with what we know. Bill Miller, a person of interest in three homicides and two probable kidnappings, just walked out of the hospital in the middle of the night. Clearly, it was a mistake to not put a uniformed officer on the guy."

Dreyfus shoots Prentiss and Cook an admonitory look and continues. "Two other suspects are nowhere to be found. Jenna Wade is a twenty year old sophomore at Glenville State who just happened to have a dead campus security guard, one Peter Dorgan, in her dorm room. Questioning of the security staff at the campus produced nothing of value. Ditto with Mrs. Dorgan, who appears as if her only concern in life is to find her way to the next bottle."

When Dreyfus pauses to stroke his chin with a look of a sage solving a centuries-old enigma, Jim Cook resists the urge to throw an empty coffee cup at him. *When he isn't stroking his ego, the son-of-a-bitch looks like he spends most of his time sniffing his own shit—and likes it.*

"Miller was pretty banged up," Cook says. "And, the thing is, I believe his story—even if he is leaving something out. The professor sure as hell isn't trying to make himself look good. He was very straightforward about his affair."

Dreyfus snorts his disapproval, and the three of them turn back to the security tape. The expression on their faces is similar—a uniform look of deep unease.

As he stares at the screen, which cycles the same two minutes of weirdness over and over, Cook thinks about the difficulty of the case. In the week before the beginning of the spring semester, it was tough to track down students appearing on the same class rosters with Ms. Wade. Campus personnel could not recall any specifics about Jenna's departure after finals week. The home address retrieved from her collegiate application turned out to be fictitious, and state and federal databases had yet to supply hits for a Mr. and Mrs. Hazael Wade—the girl's alleged parents. Her dorm roommates provided no useful information and described Jenna as bright and superficially friendly—if a little aloof. Phone records for the dorm likewise revealed nothing relevant.

And, the "Incredible-Mr.-Forked-Tongue" remained a blank slate. Apparently, no one had ever seen a guy matching Miller's description of "Gren"—other than Miller himself, of course.

Dreyfus breaks the train of Cook's thought. "Look, it's pretty obvious. Dorgan and the girl were having an affair, so Miller finds out and kills the guard in a jealous fit. At some point, Stacey Miller catches on to her husband, they fight, and Miller goes nuts and kills her and the daughter. Lendowski is maybe screwing the alluring Ms. Wade as well, so Miller guts the English professor for good measure."

"Some holes in that theory," Prentiss cuts in. "For one, there are some missing bodies. Why jump to the conclusion that the wife and daughter are dead? And, how does the lawyer, Amy Wendell, fit in?"

"Right," Cook says. "Miller doesn't seem that crazy. His story is more plausible, too: Coming to his senses, Miller dumps the girl, who gets her new boyfriend to administer revenge. Hell hath no fury like a woman scorned...."

Of course, that doesn't explain why "Gren" would go after the lawyer. She worked in the same office as Miller's wife, but what was the motive?

There's something I'm not seeing... or, maybe the killer is simply an unpredictable psycho.

Amy Wendell's mutilated body was discovered by her daughter the same night Bill left the hospital; it was the most gruesome crime scene to which Cook had ever been called. Amy's skull had been crushed. The perpetrator also violated her orally.

Cook ruminates on the case some more and stares uncomfortably at the hospital security tape.

Why would Miller leave the hospital on the sly? It makes him look guilty as hell. If he had knowledge about the whereabouts of his wife and daughter, why not tell the police? Unless... he was under duress. Maybe, following the real kidnapper's instructions?

Cook holds onto his theory for the moment. He focuses on the security video, which continues to run on a continuous loop. The seasoned detective shivers.

Damn tape freaks me out.

The video is a grainy, black and white VHS tape. At three-thirty-one a.m., on the night of January nineteen, Miller exits the emergency room doors and limps across the parking lot. Dressed in a muddy sports jacket and jeans, he soon lumbers out of sight onto the road. But, just as Miller nears the camera's outermost field of vision, a blur passes across the screen—like something *swooped in front of the camera from above.* Whatever it was, it moved too fast for the police to get a good look.

If Jim Cook had been forced to guess, and had no concerns about his professional reputation, he'd say that a giant manta ray (that flies) had launched itself off the roof of the hospital and performed a quick fly-by of the suspect as he stumbled across the parking lot.

Cook isn't forced to guess, and he isn't going to say what he thinks it looks like. Drefyus would say something impertinent, and then Cook would be up on charges for belting an FBI agent.

"A bat or bird must have flown in front of the rooftop camera." The FBI has made its official judgment, and the mystery of the swooping shadow is "solved." Only Jim Cook doesn't believe it, and neither does Jack Prentiss or Kevin Dreyfus.

Cook has worked some tough crime scenes—once locked up a woman who offered to sell her baby for fifty bucks and blow him for twenty more so she could buy crack. The detective is grounded in reality—does not believe in spooks. But, later that night, Cook dreams about the winged shape on the tape and wakes in a sweat.

"If it was a bat, then it was a really big *female* bat," he mutters. Then, the detective, who has been hardened by years of policing, alarms his disgruntled wife with a frantic nudge: he can no longer face the dark alone.

⚜ 4:2 ⚜

Jenna watches Bill march up the trail, dutifully following her instructions in the letter. From her perch forty feet up a massive beech tree, she can see Tyka moving through a mature stand of mountain laurel. The wolf springs forward to kill Bill, and Jenna commands her to halt. Unable to act outside Jenna's volition, Tyka reluctantly obeys.

Grendel slithers through the brush, already shadowing the professor's steps. Soon the two disappear over a hump of land above the cabin. Perfect—Bill stomping about the cabin would ruin her plans. *Now that Dumbshit is out of the way, I can spend some "quality time" with the females.*

Jenna is enjoying all of this, as much as she's enjoyed her sport in many years. She sits on a limb of the beech tree with her back to the massive grey trunk. A red squirrel chatters at her from a smaller branch over her head. Jenna snatches it and bites its head off. She spits out the head and slurps blood from the neck stump. Then, she tosses the tiny carcass down her throat without bothering to crunch up the bones.

Things are progressing nicely. Dumbshit breaking things off before I was finished was unexpected—but that won't change anything. Besides, that wimpy security guard was a pleasant distraction in the meantime.

When she was done feeding on the unfortunate Pete Dorgan, Jenna "received" one of her infrequent prescient visions. Brooding in her dark thought, a vision of Bill leaving his house came to her, and somehow she *knew* that he needed to stop off on his way to the campus to pick up his forgotten laptop at the hippy professor's house. The time was ripe. She dispatched Grendel with specific instructions to kill Lendowski and seize Stacey and Krista. Then, she would fly the females to the cabin while Grendel used the little boy as leverage to ensure Bill would follow instructions.

I wish I could have seen Bill's face when he discovered the body of the hippy—that would have been sweet. Such artistry in my darling boy! And, he was so ENTHUSIASTIC with the waitress and the lady lawyer. Truly admirable!

The tornado—now, that was strange. And, fortuitous. Hit just at the right moment to save Bill.

Upon questioning, Grendel admitted to Jenna that, were it not for the storm, he would have strangled Bill—contrary to her instructions. Bill dead at that juncture would have ended Jenna's "fun" prematurely.

Even now, she was not quite done with her professor.

Jenna's latest victim is clearly beginning to fade. Thinking about consuming Bill's innermost essence in their final, violent couplings makes Jenna squirm in anticipation. Her long experience tells her that the sex toward the end of the process—when her victim is physically and spiritually emaciated—will be the most fulfilling. Only then will Jenna attain satiety—for a time.

135

The woods and the shack are a perfect set-up. In another day or two—once she finishes with Bill and he is nothing more than an empty husk—Jenna will permit Grendel to tear him to pieces and feast. It will be a nice treat for her loving but increasingly wayward son.

Then, I'll turn my full attention to Stacey and Krista. I have such high hopes for those two. Such strength! Such brilliance!

Jenna stretches, grips the bark tightly with her toenails, and suspends herself upside down from the tree branch. Her thoughts turn back to Grendel. A tear forms in the corner of one eye and falls to the ground far below. As she feared, the maturation process is accelerating—an unfortunate by-product of her child's mixed parentage.

Jenna's half-human children always turn out different. Some very few, like Grendel, look human but are akin to snakes. More common are entities that resemble nothing remotely human. Many come out as hirsute bats that grow up to one-hundred-and-fifty pounds. Others look like lizards that become scaly six foot monstrosities with human eyes. Her favorites are the spiders that burst from her noxious womb in a scrambling frenzy—some of these grow to the size of dinner plates, with pincers and poisonous sting. She loves them all.

Jenna's half-human spawn normally haunt wastelands and remote areas for a few brief months. Sometimes a hunter or hiker disappears without a trace. But, always, her beloved offspring are short-lived—a fact that leaves Jenna perpetually lonely and desolate.

There are so few of her kind left, spread across the planet, and so, she mates with her children to see if she can produce a new breed that will inherit her longevity. But the ones who assume human form, and make procreation a possibility, are invariably sterile. Grendel is no exception.

My son may only have a few days left. My poor boy. My dear little filmmaker!

Jenna has not told Grendel of his imminent demise. The accelerated aging process has also produced, in the present case, a murderous rage and insanity. What Grendel will become in the end Jenna does not know for certain—perhaps a very unpredictable, anaconda-sized serpent.

Despite the few twists and uncertainties—and the regrettable but predictable situation regarding Grendel—Jenna is pleased with the progression of events. She is also confident of the outcome.

Probably won't require the wolf. Still, it was prudent. My powers aren't limitless, and it never hurts to have an extra enforcer in these situations.

Jenna hacks up the remains of the squirrel—some fur and a few sharp bones. Her thoughts turn to sex. Grendel took her around the back of the cabin not fifteen minutes ago, but incipient desire surges through her body already. *I just can't get enough.* She climbs up on the tree branch and pleasures herself with her back to the massive trunk.

A few minutes later, still breathing heavily from her exertions, Jenna thinks about Stacey and Krista. *It's time to turn my full attention to the females. They're so beautiful. Especially the little one. So much promise.*

Maybe this time, things will be different.

Jenna grips the smooth, grey bark with sharp nails and descends the tree, headfirst.

Over the next two days, Jenna divides her time between Stacey and Krista in the cabin and Bill, who she drains near to death along the forest trail. The sex is intensely satisfying—the best Jenna has experienced in many centuries.

Finally, she is done with him. Jenna celebrates by slaughtering a small deer and bathing in the warm and gushing blood. She eats the entire animal, even the bones. The transformation from her true form to twenty-year old female human consumes a large amount of energy that requires frequent feedings.

She seeks out Grendel. Jenna knows that he watched the "festivities" last night and is insanely jealous. When she finds him, she allows him to lick the deer's blood from her legs.

Grendel works his up to the cleft of Jenna's ass with his long, flickering tongue. No longer in need, Jenna slaps him away. Grendel hisses.

"I'm done with him," Jenna says. "Now, go have your way. Tear him to pieces."

Grendel rises from his knees. "Thank-you, *Mother.*"

He obediently lopes off through the mountain laurel.

Jenna summons the wolf. Tyka appears within moments. Jenna allows her to lick her hand.

You are an obedient servant. I no longer need you. Now, be free and raise havoc.

Tyka whines and is uncertain, at first. Then, her ears prick up, and she trots off.

A few minutes later, Jenna arrives at the cabin. As she descends the retractable stairs to the basement, she is overcome with another prescient vision.

A wolf tears out the throat of a man. Blood sprays in a great gout and obscures the scene in Jenna's mind's eye.

So, Tyka finished him off. Grendel will be gravely disappointed. No matter. Bill's out of the way for good. My poor Grendel will soon follow.

It's time to begin.

⊰ 4:3 ⊱

All is black. The room is cold and damp, and Krista can no longer be sure if her mommy is still there, shackled to a pipe in the corner of the cellar. The weak light from the bulb in the ceiling went out long ago.

Krista's hands and feet hurt from the extension cord that binds her. There is something like a rubber ball in her mouth, connected to a strap tied around her head. It's hard to breathe. Her throat burns, and her mouth is so dry she can barely swallow.

What if I throw up? There's no place for the puke to go!

Just when the child thinks there can be no tears left, still more trace salty trails down her cheeks. Drying pee on her legs makes her skin itch.

Something skitters across her bare feet in the dark. Krista jerks, but is unable to scream because of the gag. *Just a mouse. Just a mouse. Just a mouse.* She tries to reassure herself, but can't help imagining a forked tongue flicking softly at her ankle.

Not far away, something large shifts on the cement floor.

It must be Mommy. She probably has one of those things in her

140

mouth—that's why she can't talk to me.

Krista slips into unconsciousness—a brief respite from the fear and pain. She wakes to a cold void. There is absolutely no light. After a while, phantom shapes and colors swoop out of the dark in front of Krista's face. She closes her eyes tight, but the phantoms remain behind her eyelids.

When the physical discomfort and fear become too great, Krista retreats inside herself. She replays happier events and times in her young life. Memories of her "BFF"—Krista doesn't text, but even in kindergarten the children have picked up the contemporary cell phone lexicon—Missy Lowe, bring some comfort. Even thoughts of the disgusting Simon Drake and the less savory elements of the kindergarten class provide relief, as would any departure from the present, cruel circumstances.

As days and nights pass outside the basement of the cabin, the fragile mind of the five year old girl comes close to breaking. Krista assumes a dissociative state, where events seem to be happening to someone else who merely *looks* like her. The psychological defense mechanism is only partially effective. The psychic scars will gouge deep.

Krista replays the day Grendel came, over and over, as if she could have done something different. She wishes she had warned her mother and father about the monster who'd edged closer and closer to the house each night.

The morning after the man clung to the house right outside her window, Krista woke in her parents' bed. Jeff was barking furiously in the back yard. The barks turned to horrible howls and high-pitched screams of pain, and Krista knew that the barrier was down. The monster was coming for her.

Beneath closed and fluttering eyelids in the lightless cellar, Krista relives the horror of the day that robbed her of her childhood, and changed everything forever:

She jumps out of bed, screaming for Mommy and Daddy. It's too late—the sound of breaking glass from the French doors in the rear of the home is unmistakable. Mommy screams more horribly than Jeff, but her cry is cut short by a frightening *smack*.

Heavy steps ascend the stairs. The steps stop in front of the closed bedroom door.

Krista slides out of the bed as quickly and quietly as possible. Terrified, she hides beneath it—the only thing she can think to do. The door opens. Mud-encrusted black cowboy boots, visible beneath the hanging bedclothes, stop inches from her face. Krista covers her mouth to stifle a scream and closes her eyes tight. Eternity marked by spots and swirls behind her closed eyelids stretches on. The room is maddeningly quiet. Finally, she must open her eyes or go crazy.

The fiend stares at her under the bed from the distance of a foot. His eyes are weird—the pupils narrow and no longer perfectly round. The forked tongue flicks out and caresses Krista's cheek.

After that, the only thing the five year old remembers before regaining full consciousness in the cellar was moments of weightlessness—and a vast forest that stretched out several hundred feet below her as a bitter wind whistled in her ears.

That part must have been a dream.

Hunger gnaws at Krista's stomach. She no longer fears throwing up, because there's nothing in there. It's still completely dark. She wishes her mother would move around some so that she would know she was still there.

Krista's thoughts traverse through fear for her mother to visions of her dad, limping down a path that spans a dark, haunted woodland. Her father is heroic, tireless, and bursts into the cellar through a non-existent door to rescue them.

In the fantasy, Grendel is about to do something horrible to Stacey, but Bill appears just in time. He fights the monster and wins. They escape from the cellar and run through the forest, down the path, toward the town, people, and safety. But, Krista's troubled mind will not permit the fantasy to be fear-free: Something pursues them as they flee, grasping and threatening to kill before the family can burst through onto a paved road and flag down a passing car.

Such are Krista's thoughts, bound and gagged in the cellar of a shack, devoid of light or human touch. Unknown to the child, for much of the time her father dreams in a delirium a few feet above her head.

Just out of arm's reach on the cellar floor, her mother fights her own, desperate battle.

Waking and sleep fuse until Krista has difficulty telling them apart. She has no idea how long they've been here—wherever "here" is.

She slowly becomes aware that the blackness is no longer absolute. Her vision is filled by a uniform, red haze. Krista's mind grasps the reality: someone has turned on the light in the ceiling, which she sees through her closed eyelids.

Krista opens her eyes and blinks in pain from the forty watt illumination. She squints to get a better look.

Grendel is there, squatting right next to her on his haunches. Krista closes her eyes tight, waiting for horrible pain and death.

Nothing happens. Krista opens her eyes. Grendel hasn't moved. He just squats there on his haunches and stares at her.

Unable to do anything else, Krista takes a good look at him. He's doing something below his waist with his hand, but her eyes are drawn up to his. Grendel's eyes are no longer human. The pupils are dark, vertical slits; the irises are no longer grey, but deep gold flecked with black.

Krista is drawn into the golden depths.

She blacks out.

The next time Krista wakes, she's lying on a twin mattress. A small heater radiates warmth over her body. She looks around the cellar. Over next to a grimy toilet is Krista's mother. Stacey has two purple-yellow bruises under her eyes and a puffy, crooked nose. Dried blood stains her left cheek. Her hands are behind her back, and she has one of those gags in her mouth.

Against one wall is a large, flat-screen television. The angle isn't right, so Krista can't see what's showing.

Smack. Smack. SMACK.

The sound is from the television.

A beautiful, blonde-haired lady stands off to one side and observes Stacey as she watches the TV program. Stacey's eyes, shocked and glassy-looking, bulge out of her face.

Smack. Smack. SMACK.

A woman screams. There's a loud crash—the sound of breaking glass—followed by feeble moans. Krista is glad she can't see the TV screen—she knows from the expression on her mother's face that she wouldn't like the show either.

Why is that lady making Mommy watch TV?

SNAP.

It sounds to Krista like someone in the television program broke a small tree branch over his knee.

The pretty girl clicks a button on a remote control.

Stacey's entire body shakes with silent sobs. She has closed her eyes. When she opens them, she notices that Krista is awake.

"Krista, honey, go back to sleep," Stacey rasps. "Everything's going to be okay, sweetie."

Krista doesn't believe her mom.

I'm scared. Mommy looks really scared. And, mad. I don't understand any of this. Where's the monster?

Her mother and the lady talk quietly for a while. The lady does most of the talking.

As the conversation proceeds, Stacey gets a wild look on her face.

Stacey screams, "YOU CRAZY FUCKING *BITCH!*"

⪥ 4:4 ⪤

Everything is relative. What seems important to one person is superficial and meaningless to the next. Even within an individual's life, the circumstances that drive a person during one period often seem silly and negligible in retrospect.

Those blessed with intellect gain wisdom from perspective.

Stacey Miller has intellect. She also has wisdom and perspective—but, it has been dearly bought.

Handcuffed to a drain line next to a toilet, sitting awkwardly on the filthy cement floor of a cinder-block-walled basement, Stacey marvels at her former naiveté.

Whoever said, "ignorance is bliss" got it right. And, I embraced ignorance.

Did I really think that emotional pain from a failing marriage was as bad as things could get?

There had been a man before Bill, a graduate student she lived with for a year. It was serious, and when the break came, Stacey thought she would die. And then, when Bill strayed, that scooped out feeling hit again—like her insides were missing.

But that pain was like a pinprick compared to this. Real fear is when you fear for your life—or the life of your child.

One truth Stacey has learned is that fear can be more powerful than love—perhaps more destructive than hate. And, a black place exists beyond fear: a realm of consciousness where, if one tarries overlong, there is no return, and madness descends.

Stacey has glimpsed this place, lying in the dark, wondering if her little girl is alive or dead mere feet away on a cold, cement floor.

Despair clutches at Stacey and threatens to drag her to a light-less tomb. She fights it—for Krista's sake.

When the light comes on, a man who looks like an older version of her husband enters the basement from a retractable staircase and crouches in front of her five year old daughter. It's the beast who broke Stacey's nose and snatched them in their home.

His forked tongue flicks in and out like a snake as he watches Krista sleep. The handcuffs rattle against the metal pipe as Stacey struggles wildly.

After an eternity, the man turns from Krista and winks at Stacey. He ascends the rickety stairs and pulls them up with a clatter and a bang.

Stacey looks at Krista with desperate longing.

Utter blackness descends like a shroud.

Stacey slips in and out of consciousness. The pain in her nose makes it difficult to breathe. Real sleep comes with difficulty, and intermittently, shackled as she is, unable to lie down or get comfortable on the cold cement. The toilet bowl on which she rests her head reeks. Exhaustion brings minimal relief on those occasions when she does drift off, because nightmares stalk her unconscious mind.

She has no memory of arriving in the cellar—no clear conception of how long they've been here.

Has it been a day? A week?

Consciousness and unconsciousness meld together.

The low hum of a motor breaks the silence from time to time. When the motor runs, the forty watt bulb comes on, and a space heater removes some of the chill from the basement.

Sounds like an electric generator. We must be in the middle of nowhere. At least the freak is keeping us from freezing to death. Keeping us alive—but, for what purpose?

One time, the cellar remains dark for what seems like an especially long period. The air becomes deeply cold. Just when her bladder feels like it's going to burst, Stacey hears the hum of the generator. The overhead bulb comes on. The retractable stairs in the ceiling unfold with a loud creak and bang.

The maniac tromps down the stairs and grins at Stacey.

Stacey makes muffled sounds through the gag in her mouth. To her surprise, he walks over and takes out the gag.

"What do you need, honey? A good fuck?"

Stacey thinks about screaming, but incorrectly intuits no one would hear her.

"Please, let me go to the bathroom."

"Sure, as long as I can watch."

Grendel takes out a small metal pin and releases Stacey from the cuffs. She has an impulse to go for his throat.

No, he'll kill me easy. I need a weapon.

The pain in her bladder overcomes her reticence. She rises stiffly and sits on the toilet. Grendel crouches down right in front of her. The whole time she goes, his mutilated tongue flicks in and out. An enormous erection is clearly visible through his jeans.

After Grendel gags her and shackles her with the handcuffs again, he goes over and stares at Krista while she sleeps.

NO. NO. NO! Stacey struggles wildly. The handcuffs rattle and grate.

Grendel squats next to Krista for a while and flicks his tongue. He takes out his swollen penis. The head is the size and color of a ripe plum. He strokes himself slowly at first, then faster.

Please, don't wake up, sweetie.

Krista wakes up. She looks frightened at first, but then she just stares in Grendel's face as if hypnotized.

He never touches her.

Before he ejaculates, Grendel looks up at the ceiling like someone called for him—though Stacey heard no sound or voice.

Clearly disappointed, the monster creaks up the steps and pulls them up after him.

The generator continues to hum. Stacey takes the opportunity to visually examine Krista. It looks like she passed out again.

What must she be thinking? What did that monster do with Billy? Is my little boy still alive? Where the hell is Bill?

When she thinks of her husband—who dreams in a fever just over her head—Stacey grits her teeth. She knows it's irrational, but on some level, she blames Bill for the situation.

When the generator stops and the light goes off, Stacey breathes in the utter blackness and void of the basement like it's a tangible thing. She envisions the pale face of her beautiful daughter.

She doesn't even look like a real girl anymore. More like a pale, lifeless doll in a little blue dress. She's dying.

My little girl is slowly dying.

Despair threatens to rise and smother her. Instead, Stacey embraces fear.

The fear evolves into a rising tide of emotion that becomes an overpowering, primal hatred.

Stacey resolves to scratch out Grendel's eyes the next time he takes off the cuffs.

I'll do whatever it takes. Suck his cock. I don't care. As long as I get a chance. The next time he takes off the cuffs.

If there is a next time.

When the light comes on again, it's not Grendel who descends the steps into the basement.

A very attractive young woman Stacey has never seen before walks over and picks up Krista.

⊰ 4:5 ⊱

The young woman does not seem to belong in a damp and grey basement filled with years of cobwebs and musty decay. Stacey is surprised, confused, and frightened, and would rub her eyes in disbelief if her hands were not handcuffed to a pipe behind her back.

She does not dare to hope, even if the pleasant and smiling face of the girl is a welcome reprieve from the man who calls himself Grendel. She can't be more than twenty-three with blonde hair, blue eyes, and perfectly tight body in jeans and blue sweater—a knockout.

The woman removes Krista's bonds and gag and carries her over to a mattress on the floor by the space heater. Krista stirs and moans, but she remains asleep.

What is this? Where's the freak?

Jenna gently strokes Krista's cheek and walks over to Stacey. She removes the gag.

"Please, please, help my daughter," Stacey cries. "She's just a baby. Please, help her!"

"I'll save her," Jenna replies with calm assurance. "She's far too important to me. As are you, Stacey."

Jenna gets down on the floor in front of Stacey and crosses her legs underneath herself like a swami. She smiles reassuringly. Stacey thinks she's the most beautiful woman she's ever seen.

The truth hits Stacey like a kick in the gut. *It's her. The one Bill was screwing.*

Hope of rescue deflates like an old, discarded tire.

"Yes, I'm the one," Jenna says, correctly interpreting the look on Stacey's face. "Your husband was a treat. Honestly, though, there's not much more to him than a hunk of meat attached to a decent erection.

"If it's any consolation, the pleasure I got from fucking him was mostly because I knew he loved you. But, I still got him to betray you. Get it?"

"Yeah, I get it," Stacey rasps. "You're a fucking bitch."

Jenna laughs. "Too true. I am."

"What in God's name do you want?" Stacey cries. "Why are you doing this to us? Look at my little girl. She's dying!"

"I told you—that's not going to happen. You can't see it yet, but putting you and Krista through all of this was necessary.

"I've found that, if you want someone to make a radical choice, you have to break them down first—whittle away all of the pretense and bullshit until you get to the core. Call it refinement by fire.

"We're going to find out who you really are, Stacey."

What the hell is she talking about? She's as nutty as the freak!

Jenna rises and climbs the steps. Stacey can hear her walking around above her head over the hum of the generator. A couple of minutes later, Jenna returns with various items. She covers Krista with a blanket. Then, she holds a cup of cool water while Stacey sips. It feels so good, Stacey resists the impulse to spit the fluid in Jenna's face.

"Please, just tell me what you want. I'll do anything if you let my daughter go."

"Be patient," Jenna replies. "The answers are coming. There's one more thing you need to see. Then, you'll have to make a very important decision."

Jenna hollers up the steps, "Bring it down!"

Grendel struggles awkwardly down the steps with a large, flat screen television. He makes another trip up and back, and within minutes the TV and a DVD player are set up and plugged in to the same socket as the space heater.

Incredulous, Stacey just watches.

Oh, good. I can catch up on Mad Men.

Stacey emits a wild cackle—a phantom of genuine laughter.

Grendel glances over at her and smiles. "That's the spirit, sweetheart!"

Stacey does a double-take. *What's wrong with his eyes?*

Jenna says, "I forgot the popcorn, but now it's time for the movie of the week. I call it, 'Grendel Beats a Nice Lawyer Lady to Death.'"

Jenna turns on the TV and inserts a disc in the DVD-player. Grendel tromps up the steps. He's seen this feature before—is the star of the show.

The blank screen jumps from nothing to an extreme close-up of Grendel's face. He grins with ill-concealed malice. When he pulls back from the camera, Stacey immediately recognizes the living room of Amy's condo.

Amy lies on the couch. She is naked, bound, and gagged. Her eyes are huge, frightened ovals.

Grendel strides over to Amy and takes out his engorged penis. Eyes bulging, Amy shakes her head violently. Grendel slaps her hard across the face. He grabs a wave of auburn hair at the back of her head and yanks her into an upright position. With his free hand, Grendel takes off the gag.

"Please," Amy cries, but she is cut off.

Grendel rams his penis into her mouth. Still holding on to the back of her head with one hand, he thrusts into her face violently for several minutes. His pumping, muscular ass blocks the view so that Stacey can't see her friend's face.

That's some shoddy camera work. The thought shoots through Stacey's head, and she realizes that, for the moment, she's teetering on the brink of insanity.

When Grendel finishes, Stacey thinks that Amy is dead. He's released some of his spunk across her face. One cheek is swollen from his vicious slap.

A single tears slides down Stacey's cheek.

On the screen, Grendel shakes Amy roughly by the shoulder.

"Wake up, honey. We're not done."

Amy moans and opens her eyes.

"Please…"

Smack. Holding her by the back of the head with his left hand, Grendel slaps Amy across the face with his right—hard.

Smack—a backhand connects with Amy's other cheek.

SMACK. Amy's head rocks violently.

Smack. Smack. SMACK.

After a minute, Amy's face is no longer recognizable.

Stacey finally looks away.

"Huh," says Grendel on the TV. "This cunt's a tough one."

Stacey looks back to the screen in time to see Grendel pick Amy up like a sack of potatoes and toss her body against the wall. A mirror shatters. The couch blocks the view, so Stacey can't see Amy where she has landed on the floor.

Grendel strides over behind the couch and raises a size eighteen cowboy boot. He tromps down hard, and there is a sickening *crunch*.

Jenna turns off the TV with a click of the remote and turns to examine Stacey.

Stacey's chin rests on her upper chest. Her body hitches with quiet sobs.

Jenna giggles.

"Stacey, let's have a chat. I think you're ready, now.

"I'm sure you've been wondering—your son is fine and being treated like a celebrity in the Braddock County hospital. Bill is dead. Thought you should know. The big scary guy with the tongue is my son, fathered by your husband. Big for a four month old, isn't he?"

She's insane. Bill cheated on me with a beautiful, insane twit.

Stacey wants to believe the news about Billy. Somehow, she does not believe that Bill is dead. She dares to hope, but her mind won't let go of the images of Amy being raped and murdered.

The insane girl continues to speak. She's not making much sense, but Stacey listens and tries to glean whatever useful information she might be able to use.

"For now, you can call me Jenna. I've had many names over

the millennia. I'm a creature, Stacey. Not human—both spirit and flesh. I feed off human misery and despair. Sex with individuals I've drained psychically is the best, though."

"Just tell me what you want," Stacey says, sounding exhausted and resigned.

"Okay," Jenna says, rubbing her palms together. "Here it is: I'm lonely. Ages ago, there were hundreds of entities like me running around—some male, some female. But, now, my kindred are spread very thin. I don't know why. Sometimes, I think it's because this unimaginative world can't conceive of things like me, and that makes it less possible for my kind to thrive.

"Some written stories and oral traditions call us succubi and incubi. But, the stories don't do justice to the reality. 'Nephalim' is another term I've heard, and I think that's closer to the truth.

"Anyhow, if you haven't guessed, I want you, and especially Krista, to join me—become like me. You would no longer be fully human, of course.

"I know you think I'm insane, Stacey, but it's all true. Just imagine enjoying centuries of unrestrained sexual pleasure as have I— and true love unblemished by foolish guilt!"

Jenna pauses and licks her lips provocatively—slow and sensual.

Stacey watches Jenna throughout the soliloquy. She is incredulous and unsure of how to respond to someone who is clearly deranged. Knowing that the correct response might save the life of her daughter, Stacey is nevertheless unable to say anything but what pops into her mind:

"So, let me get this straight. You're a hoar whore?"

Jenna laughs—not a witch's cackle, but a soft and pleasant

sound, like the tinkling of wind chimes, or the fall of a gentle spring rain.

"Oh, I *do* like you Stacey," she says. "Word play is one of my favorite games outside of sex. I just *knew* I made the right choice!"

Stacey has heard enough. She thinks of Amy, and Krista, and the rage that has been building inside of her bursts forth like an erupting volcano.

She screams at Jenna: "YOU CRAZY FUCKING BITCH!"

Jenna just grins. "Still don't believe, Stacey?

"I've seen this disbelief many times before. But, it still intrigues me—this inability of your kind to break free from the cage of reason and consider the possibility of realities beyond your comprehension."

Jenna begins to pace the cellar.

"Hell, the prevailing wisdom of your most respected thinkers holds that the life on this planet evolved from single-celled organisms into only *one* intelligent life form. How incredibly narrow-minded!"

Jenna laughs her musical laugh again—no one would ever suspect it emanated from an entirely inhuman soul.

"Or, here's a good one on the origins of the universe: galaxies beyond counting with an incomprehensibly large mass—with vast parsecs of space separating them—are generated from a cosmic explosion billions of years ago. There is no explanation for the impetus of the bang, or the enigma of a gargantuan amount of matter emanating from nothingness. And yet, your purveyors of *science* arrogantly proclaim they've solved the great mysteries!

"Why box yourself in, Stacey? Why fail to recognize the limitless possibilities of our existence?"

Jenna pauses when she sees the seething rage emanating from Stacey.

Good. She's ready.

Smiling to herself with unconcealed glee, Jenna knows the right moment has arrived. She says, "There are more things in heaven and earth—to quote your beloved Bard. But, I digress.

"And so, Stacey, I present the antidote to your puerile incredulity."

Jenna licks her lips like an animal in anticipation of a long-awaited meal. She stands and begins to undress. Stacey is relieved to see that Krista has gone back to sleep.

Jenna stands naked in front of Stacey, smiling triumphantly. Her jeans and sweater lay in a heap about her feet.

She may be crazy, but that body is perfect. Air-brushed Playboy bunnies don't look that good. No wonder Bill couldn't resist. I hate her.

"Are you ready, Stacey?" Jenna asks with a lascivious grin. Here we go."

The next thing that happens will forever rob Stacey of a piece of her sanity—a place in the nightmare recesses of her mind where the potential for future love, or hope, is mitigated.

The hum of the generator becomes muted. The light from the forty watt bulb grows dim. Shadows creep from the corners of the cellar. Jenna's angelic face *melts* into the visage of a green hag with scaly skin and long black hair. The eyes are the worst—pus-yellow, with large vacant pupils.

A black tongue comes out to lick bluish lips that look like dead worms. Four yellow incisors protrude from either side of the stench-filled mouth. Something like vast bat wings sprout from its naked back—the flesh there is a mottled grey, and corpse-like.

It's just a flash bulb of a moment: no more than a few seconds before the light bulb returns full force and a smiling, beautiful, *human-looking* Jenna stands in front of Stacey.

In that interval, Stacey screams. And, screams. And, screams.

☙ 4:6 ❧

Krista wakes when her mother shrieks. The child leaps to her feet and runs to Stacey.

Jenna is in human form—still naked with arms folded under full, perky breasts.

Krista buries her face in Stacey's blood-stained blouse.

With lips already tingling from hyperventilation, Stacey manages a few breathless words of comfort as Krista wets her blouse with tears.

Stacey is a fighter like her mother. She desperately clings to her sanity.

That was real. That really happened.

She finally gathers the courage to look at Jenna. "You want us to become like *you?* How is that even possible? And what if I refuse?"

Jenna is pleased that Stacey has accepted the reality of her situation. *Not many of them progress this far without totally losing it.* She says, "Still hung up on possibilities, Stacey? No? I didn't think so.

"To answer question *numero uno...* It's a long process that will take several years. You and Krista will become like me as we share knowledge of ourselves. This is accomplished through a mingling of our innermost being. Of course, the process is most expeditiously and efficaciously accomplished through... hmmmmm, how shall I put this to you?

"Okay, got it! The three of us will enjoy... *carnal pursuits.*"

Jenna continues: "As for question *numero dos*: I'd rather not do it, but I've been thinking about allowing my artistic son to star in and direct a sequel to his first feature film. I think we'll call it: 'Man with Giant Cock Rapes the Shit out of Little Girl While Mommy Watches.' Not a very catchy title, but I know some audiences that will *absolutely love it.*

"Think it over, Stace."

Jenna puts her clothes back on and is just a perfectly built and stunningly beautiful young woman again. Krista still has her face buried in her mother's midsection. Jenna climbs the rickety wooden stairs and pulls them up after her.

Stacey can hear her walking around up there for a minute or two.

Now, there's only the muffled hum of the generator. Stacey wishes she could put her arms around Krista.

"We're going to make it outta' here, sweetie," Stacey says. But, she doesn't really believe it.

Just before the light bulb goes dark and leaves Krista and Stacey in inky, chill blackness, Stacey sees a tiny glitter of hope on the basement floor.

Part V

The Trail

Tyka watches Bill as he stumbles up the path.   Grendel, worming his way through the brush on his belly, is not far off to the right of the trail.

The wolf trails the man, who still smells faintly of dog, for two days. She steers clear of Grendel. The man finally collapses at the base of a cliff.

That night, Tyka's master descends on the man again and again. Grendel is nearby. Tyka emits a series of whimpers as the black rage radiating from Grendel intensifies.

The next day, Jenna calls Tyka. Jenna speaks to her mind and tells her that she is no longer necessary. The Tunku releases Tyka and suggests that she sew death and discord in the woods.

Now, the wolf becomes conscious of something entirely new— it's as if she's been confined in a cage all of her life, but did not realize it until now. With the last command—one of release and dismissal—Jenna instills in Tyka the greatest boon of the three conferred attributes.

The first gift was consciousness and the ability to interpret emotions as do humans; the second, the desire for human flesh; and, the last—free will.

Self-awareness, a human capacity to feel and interpret anger, pity, fear—even love—and, now, freedom to do as she will.

Tyka is a new and unique entity.

She searches for the only thing still missing: a purpose.

The wolf sniffs the air. Yes. There they are—not far.

Her sense of smell is so extraordinary that she can still detect a whiff of Jeff coming from both of them. She feels pity for the poor animal who was so brutally murdered.

Tyka bounds off in pursuit of Bill and Grendel.

ill walks down the path that leads deep into the Black
Moshannon. The temperature has climbed into the low
50s. Most of the snow cover has melted. Patches of
white like cotton gauze remain on north-facing slopes and in the
shadows of the boulders strewn about.

If there is a God—the possibility seems especially remote at this
point—Bill thinks that maybe He's decided to be merciful for a
little while. The January sunshine on his face feels divine.

Lord, a REAL miracle right now would be a double cheeseburger and
fries.

Bill feels only slightly guilty at his irreverence. His stomach
feels caved in, and he's thinking seriously about chewing on some
tree bark.

It's the second day since the shack. Bill had no trouble picking
up the trail. He's followed the path for many miles now—or, so
he believes. The fever and its delirium have returned, and Bill's
judgment is severely impaired.

In all this time, he's actually traveled little more than three quarters of a mile from the cabin.

Bill stumbles on, growing weaker with each step. Remarkably, no candy wrappers, empty water bottles, or paint blazes herald the existence of civilization. Bill almost expects to come face-to-face with an equally startled Ohio Indian around the next bend in the trail.

There is no wind. The woods are preternaturally silent.

Bill believes he is utterly alone.

Sudden thoughts occasionally pierce the fog of pain and fever.

Does Krista have her winter coat? Is Stacey really dead? Who's watching over Big Billy? Is he with Issy? And, just what the hell am I doing bumbling along this trail to nowhere? I think I've made some very foolish decisions recently. Beginning with the one where I left the hospital in the middle of the night.

The forest trail becomes like a tunnel—just brown winter walls with patches of white on either side. The faces of Bill's family appear at the end. They seem to retreat from him down the darkening tunnel, always out of reach.

Part of Bill's physical and mental weakness is due to troubled sleep. The previous night, he curled up beneath two huge boulders that leaned together and provided a remarkably dry shelter. But, he also experienced some very disturbing dreams—not unlike the ones that plagued him last fall.

Bill begins to suspect that the purpose of his hike through the forest is simply to make him suffer. He begins to doubt he will see Stacey and Krista again—at least, not alive. Would the next rise and dip in the endless trail reveal their bodies, cruelly left there for him to discover?

Seething hatred for Jenna and Grendel propel him forward.

Tyka and Grendel, watching from separate areas of thick cover the previous night, observed Bill as he slept. The wolf and the serpent witnessed a dense, filmy shadow stoop over Bill on several occasions. Each time, the unmistakable but weirdly out-of-place sounds of sexual intercourse rose from the writhing shadows.

Toward evening of the second day from the cabin, Bill drinks deeply from a small spring that trickles from under a moss-covered boulder. The elements, the physical trials his body has been through, and the psychic drain from the thing that stalks his dreams have reduced the professor to a walking shell.

The spring water revives him a little. He limps forward and barely sees the grey boulders, mountain laurel, and giant oaks that line the path. Bill begins to wonder just how big the Black Moshannon is—thinking in his denuded state that he has traveled far from the shack.

Clouds thickened all day, and now, the forest dims in premature twilight. The air grows chilly.

It might snow tonight. If it does, I'm a goner.

A ruffed grouse explodes out of the brush on the side of the trail. Bill wishes he could plunk it with a stone. He's so hungry he thinks he'd eat it raw, feathers and all. The bird is far too quick—gone in a heartbeat.

Bill rounds a bend in the trail and is afforded a breath-taking view of the Little Kittanning River eight hundred feet below. The path in this spot has come very close to the edge of a precipice. Vertigo seizes Bill as he looks over the edge straight down to a cluster of boulders far below.

He moves on. Around another bend, a rock face rises straight up eighty feet on the right side of the trail. A narrow shelf slants across this cliff face about a third of the way up. A fall of rocks at the base and to one side could be climbed with some effort if one desired to reach the shelf. It's an intriguing prospect, as a dark triangle in the middle of the narrow walkway suggests a small cave or shelter.

A patch of snow whitens the ground at the base of the cliff. Bill eats several handfuls to satisfy his thirst.

Bill sits with his back to the rock wall. The forest is silent except for the occasional croak of a passing crow. Bill begins to cry. The moments of absolute faith he experienced in the previous weeks seem to mock him. The possibility of "God" is very remote.

Unbidden, an image of Jenna appears to his mind's eye—not the nasty whore who deserves death, but the lovely and charming young woman he'd had sex with dozens of times. Bill wonders how he could have been so blind—and, so selfish.

I screwed up. Again. What the hell am I doing? Why in God's name would I do anything Jenna tells me to do? I should have gone straight for the nearest road as soon as I got out of the cabin—even if it meant re-crossing the river. Let the police take over. Hell, I have Jenna's letter—a confession from a lunatic. If I went back to the road, the state police could be combing the shack for clues and searching the forest from the air by now.

Bill lies down at the base of the cliff and cries some more. The fever returns with new ferocity. His mind and body are near the breaking point. Thoughts scurry about in a disjointed blur. He barely has enough strength to raise his head.

Thinking about Jenna's explanation regarding "Grendel," Bill imagines he's slipped through a crack in reality and landed in another dimension. He rolls onto his back and stares unseeing at the somber sky.

Maybe there are supernatural forces at work.

Bill hums the theme to the *Twilight Zone*—then, laughs wearily and without mirth. It is a hoarse cackle from a half-crazed man.

A bobcat in the cave above wakes and pricks up its ears at so strange a sound.

Too tired to climb the fall of rocks to the ledge and the small cave—the bobcat might not have given up her abode without a fight in any event—Bill crawls beneath a slight overhang at the base of the cliff.

Scant shelter, but at least it's dry.

For Bill, the end of all endurance and suffering is very near.

⚜ 5:2 ⚜

At the top of the precipice, Grendel looks down at his prey. He is not happy, having stalked his father for two days.

Mother should be satisfied by now. It's time to bring this business to a close. And feast.

Grendel contemplates a climb down the cliff to end things right here.

No, I have to wait. Mother would be displeased if I consumed him before she's done.

Twilight deepens. A starless night arrives, and the temperature drops ten degrees.

Grendel lies on his stomach at the cliff's edge with his head resting on his arms. He watches Bill sleep eighty feet below. His father just lies under the overhang like a dead thing, hour after hour.

Sometime after midnight, Grendel senses that he is no longer alone. A mist and a shadow appear at the base of the cliff, not far from Bill.

A few minutes later, Grendel hears Bill grunt and moan. Silence settles for a half an hour, and then it starts up again. After a long time, Bill climaxes with a prolonged, shuddering groan.

The sound of coitus is so loud that some critter takes off through the underbrush.

The cycle repeats itself—four more times throughout the night. Watching the action from above, Grendel clenches his melon-sized fists. He is mad with jealousy and hatred.

Grendel's sense of hearing and sight are as good as a cat's, and his nose is as keen as any dog's—but, he is not aware of Jenna's presence until she whispers in his ear.

"Hello, Lover."

She's covered with the blood of an animal. Grendel immediately begins to lick the tacky fluid from her legs. But, when he tries to stick his tongue in her ass, she slaps him away.

Grendel is furious. He barely restrains a sudden impulse to attack her. But, then, Jenna says what he's been waiting weeks to hear.

"I'm done with him. Now, go have your way. Tear him to pieces."

☙ 5:3 ❧

Bill wakes from a troubled sleep. His first sight is of the rock overhang and the grey cliff that rises sheer above his head. The night before had been snow and frost-free again, but his body shakes with uncontrollable shivering.

He contemplates sitting up—even makes an effort—but quickly changes his mind. The mere thought of movement weighs Bill down as if the strong hands of a giant are planted firmly in the middle of his chest.

This is nuts. I've got to turn back. I probably can't make it now, but at least I can try.

Having made a rational decision, Bill takes a deep breath, rises, and discovers that he has some strength remaining after all.

Bill does not notice the small sounds of movement from the top of the cliff.

In a few minutes, he arrives at the overlook he passed on the previous day. The Little Kittanning River lies at the base of the gorge like a winding, silver ribbon. The day is brightening, and since he is already exhausted, Bill chooses to stop at the rock overhang and take in the sight.

A shaft of light through breaking morning clouds spotlights a raging whitewater that appears to Bill far above as gentle silver ripples. He didn't appreciate it before, but the scene is quite special. Tears come to his eyes.

Bill is overcome with a sense of confidence and well-being. The experience is less like feeling than belief. He felt like this twice before: once, on the ride over to Steve's house before he discovered his body, and again at Billy's bedside in the hospital.

Bill believes he hears a voice speak to him from a place deep inside: *Trust me. I AM in control.*

Bill falls to his knees. The moment is sublime, and the broken man sobs with relief as he suddenly understands there will be no more ambivalence—no more doubt.

Bill prays: "Please, God, please, God, please, God, help me; help my family."

He lays down flat on his stomach with his cheek pressed to the cool rock—broken at last.

Grendel pursues his father as he makes his way back toward the rock overlook. It had taken him several minutes after Jenna gave him the go-ahead for Grendel to descend the treacherous cliff face. Now, he easily diminishes the gap between him and his prey.

The sight of his father, a hundred yards down the trail, makes Grendel sick. *He's so weak and pathetic. Aside from the looks, I'm glad I take after Mother.*

Mother is everything to Grendel—is all he really loves, or cares to love. It is a possessive love, and why not? Jezebel (her real name) is all he has ever known.

He was born in the shack. From there, Mother taught him to hunt in the forest, and it was her soft voice that told him stories of past times and civilizations. His mother's affair with the Emperor Nero, and her part in the fire that devastated Rome, was one of his favorites. Even as a child, he was aroused by these bloody tales of human depravity that fostered his education and lulled him to sleep.

She introduced him to sex when he was six weeks old and had matured into the form of an adolescent human. This brief time was when Grendel experienced unblemished happiness. But, then, his mother began to disappear for long passages of time. She told him he must remain in the woods.

Grendel used the solitude of his youth to explore the forest. He ran the woods at night and tore the throats out of whitetail fawns. But, he missed Mother—some of the larger woodland animals he buggered were a poor substitute for *her* embrace.

During Jenna's long absences, his lust became a torment. He wanted to stick his penis in everything. If the object, living or dead, didn't have an orifice—or an orifice large enough—he'd tear it a new hole. He wanted to fuck *the world*.

Then, Mother finally returned. She told him about his father and of her plans for Bill's human family. Jealous and hurt, Grendel was consoled when she finally turned him loose.

I enjoyed tearing the arms off that pretty waitress. Gutting the sniveling, hippy professor and doing that cunt of a lawyer was almost as much fun as screwing Mother. And, now, I'll kill Father. Rip open his belly and fuck his corpse.

Bill disappears around a bend in the trail just yards ahead of Grendel.

The monster, sporting a throbbing erection, closes in.

I've grown stronger than even Mother knows. When I finish here, I'll ravage and devour the females in the cabin. Then, I'll rape Mother— strangle her near to death as I come. She'll like that.

Grendel doesn't know his unnatural metabolism leaves him with only a few days to live.

He watches Bill collapse at the brink of the gorge. For a moment, he fears that he's been robbed of the pleasure of the kill.

Stealthy as a cat, Grendel strides forward to the precipice. Bill lies on his face, motionless. His back slowly rises and falls.

Good. He's still alive. The meat is always so much better dripping and fresh off the bone.

❧ 5:4 ❧

Jim Cook strides down the old logging road, flanked by a crusty dude named Tim Stains and a Glenville borough police rookie, Cody Gulikowski. They are not the best company for a four mile hike. Tim smells of stale beer and three day old (or three week old?) sweat, and Cody is a hopeless Serpico-wannabee at the seasoned age of twenty-two.

The FBI doesn't tag along, and that's just fine with Cook. This woodland jaunt is probably a waste of time.

Then again, it wouldn't be the first time we got lucky and solved a crime on a hunch.

Jenna Wade is still a mystery, as is "Gren." The description of the chief suspect in the murder of two people as having a forked tongue and looking quite a bit like one of the witnesses (or suspect) makes Cook think that maybe they should be looking for a one-armed man as well.

Questioning of campus students and staff turned up zilch on "Gren," and the FBI database of known aliases was equally nonproductive. The home address on Jenna's college application was an empty warehouse in Belle Vernon, Ohio. Her social security number belongs to a woman reported missing years ago.

On a whim, Cook Googled "Hazael" (Jenna's father's first name, recorded on her college application), and turned up a not-so-savory character from the Old Testament of the Bible. On a lark, Cook even looked up the name "Grendel" and discovered a synopsis of the story *Beowulf*—more useless information.

The girl's tuition—and *damn* was she good-looking in her student ID photo—had been paid directly from a numbered account in the Cayman Islands. The FBI was working on the Cayman authorities and their bank secrecy laws, but that was going to take some time.

In the meantime, Cook uses his imagination:

Question: *Why would Bill Miller leave the hospital in the middle of the night?*

Answer: *He was contacted by his family's kidnappers and foolishly followed their instructions to bypass the police and proceed to the Black Moshannon Forest.*

Question: *What the hell is in the Black Moshannon Forest?*

Answer: *A lot of trees and a plethora of woodland critters, who, smarter than a dozen police authorities searching the woods, are holed up for the winter in their dens... And, maybe, just maybe, some sort of shelter deep in the forest where a kidnapped mother and daughter might be kept far from prying eyes?*

Cook learned a long time ago that being a detective means considering all sorts of things—including remote and unlikely possibilities.

Leaving behind the image of a new species of giant bat or flying manta ray that swooped in front of the hospital security camera, Cook decided to consult with some locals. That brought him to the dilapidated patch house of the ill-smelling, unemployed, but Black Moshannon-knowledgeable Tim Stains.

"Hell yeah, there's a shack out there on the Calumet side of the river," Stains said. "It's about four miles out an old logging road growed up with scrub oaks and locusts, but some yokels still go out there every now and then to party and screw. For a case of Rolling Rock, I'll take you there."

So here they are, hiking down an old logging road on the east bank of the Little Kittanning River.

The shadows under the trees and the wind whistling through the branches do not speak to the detective of a "wild goose chase." Jim Cook's hackles are up.

Cook carries a Glock .357-sig. A round is chambered, and fifteen hollow points are in the clip. He removes the gun from its holster.

Probably nothing out here. But, why take chances?

Cook hushes Stains and the deputy, who haven't stopped jabbering since they set out. He scans the moss-laced boulders and bracken to either side of the path. Here and there, a patch of snow still lingers in the shadows. All is silent. The river itself seems muted.

An inhuman shriek echoes through the woods. The sound of animals in combat follows. The commotion is some distance off—perhaps a mile.

Cook leads the way down the trail at a quick trot.

What sounds like a dog emits a series of shrieking yelps.

Silence returns. Even the wind hushes.

The men hurry forward.

Over a shoulder of the ridge, a ribbon of grey smoke rises. When they come around the next bend in the path, Cook gets a glimpse of an old cabin through the thick tree stems.

B ill lies on his face. Slowly, the feeling of being draped in a warm cocoon fades.

Grendel walks casually up to Bill. He has a throbbing erection. He grabs Bill by the neck with one hand and yanks him off the ground.

Sharp, filthy nails clamp down on Bill's throat like a vise. Bill looks into Grendel's golden snake eyes and knows him as his son.

Grendel hisses in triumph: "Got you, *bitch!*"

The last thing Bill sees before a black curtain descends over his vision is Grendel's gaping mouth lunging toward his throat.

This is going to hurt.

An animal snarls—it sounds like an attacking dog.

The pressure on Bill's neck disappears.

When his vision returns a few moments later, Bill sees Grendel rolling around on the ground and struggling with a large, grey animal. Bill thinks it's a Siberian Husky, but then recognizes Tyka for what she is.

Grendel is on his back. Tyka snaps at his throat but comes up just short. Grendel grabs a double-handful of fur about the wolf's neck and pushes her up and away.

Tyka claws deep, red furrows in Grendel's face. Grendel screams but doesn't release Tyka from his grip.

With inhuman strength, Grendel rises to his feet and hurls the wolf twenty feet through the air. Tyka smashes against the trunk of an oak tree and collapses at its base.

Teeth bared, Tyka rises.

She moves slowly forward with a guttural snarl. Grendel pulls a red object from his jeans pocket. Tyka leaps. Grendel falls over backwards with Tyka on top. Her fangs snap an inch from his throat. Grendel strikes the flare that he holds and thrusts it into Tyka's side.

Bill looks around frantically for a rock or stick as the smell of burning animal hair fills his nostrils. The odor is sickening. Tyka's yelps of agony are worse.

Grendel rises from the ground to watch Tyka burn. She's running around in circles, the fur on her side aflame.

Grendel throws his head back and laughs.

On legs that feel like toothpicks, Bill rises for what he figures is the last time and jumps on Grendel's back. Grendel shrugs his shoulders and twists his body. Bill flies off to the side.

Grendel strides to where Bill has fallen at the brink of the gorge.

This is it. I'm dead.

A grey, smoking blur flies at Grendel. Tyka closes her fangs on Grendel's thick neck. Blood shoots from his throat in a crimson spray.

Darkness falls across Bill's vision. Just before he passes out, he smiles at the last thing he sees.

Grendel is flat on his back. Tyka tears at his throat.

Grendel's head almost comes off.

Something is nuzzling Bill's throat.

It's the wolf, as gentle as a mother calling a kindergartner for his first day of school.

Jenna imbued Tyka with three unique gifts. With the last—freewill—Tyka made a choice. Motivated by the pity she felt for the murdered dog, Jeff, she decided to save the animal's *Tunku*.

Tyka licks Bill's face.

Bill raises his head a little.

What does it want?

Raw, red-black skin shows through patches of burnt hair on the animal's left flank. She pokes harder at Bill with her snout, intent on communicating her will.

At last, Bill gets the idea. He grabs the fur on the side that isn't injured. Bill climbs until he lies on his stomach across the muscular frame of the animal.

Surprised at nothing, Bill looks back over his shoulder as the wolf takes off at a trot back down the trail toward the cabin.

The flare that burned Tyka has set some leaves and dead brush on fire next to the path. Grendel lies near the scenic overlook, his legs twisted under him at an unnatural angle. Bill guesses that he must have grown to about seven feet.

About Grendel's body, a large pool of spreading blood glistens in the sunlight beaming down from above.

⚜ 5:6 ⚜

"**K**rista, baby, Mommy loves you, but I need you to do something for me, *right now!*"

Stacey whispers the hurried words in her daughter's ear in case Jenna is listening upstairs.

Krista is terrified—reluctant to leave her mother now that they have finally been reunited.

Stacey becomes stern. She feels like a bitch for doing it, but she *commands* Krista to do as she says.

Krista is weary of being afraid of the dark. She fears some critter will scurry across her hands as she crawls across the basement floor. The basement is pitch black.

Finally, she does what her mother says. Expecting at any moment to be grabbed by Grendel—who was hiding in the shadows of the basement all along—Krista crawls forward on her hands and knees.

Grendel does not grab her. After crawling back and forth for a few terrifying minutes, Krista feels the tiny piece of metal her mother said was there.

The small metal object is a handcuff key.

Just before the generator shut off and they were plunged into total dark, Stacey saw it glittering on the floor near where Jenna had piled her clothes—it must have fell out of a pocket when she disrobed to change into the "Hag from Hell."

Stacey doesn't believe in miracles, but has no problem exploiting incredible strokes of luck. She explains to Krista how the cuffs work. There must be a tiny hole for the pin to go into.

Minutes seem to stretch out for hours. Stacey expects Jenna or Grendel to return at any moment. She offers encouraging words and wills herself to sound composed and relaxed for Krista's benefit.

"Mommy, I can't."

"Keep trying, baby. Keep trying."

Stacey waits for the hum of the generator. It doesn't come.

The cuffs click open.

Stacey staggers to her feet and falls when her numb legs betray her. She rubs them, willing the blood to restore nerve sensation.

"Let's go." Stacey grabs Krista's hand. They take baby steps toward where the stairs fold down. Blindly waving one hand in the air, Stacey finds and grasps the hanging cord that will pull the stairs down.

A terrifying clank and screech alerts anyone within three hundred yards that they are attempting an escape. The stairs unfold. A dank rug tumbles down. Dazzling morning light—only a dull grey coming through dirty windows—momentarily blinds Stacey.

Leading Krista up the steps, Stacey pokes her head into the main room of the cabin. Her breath comes in shallow, rapid gasps. Cool, clammy sweat beads her forehead. Any second now, she expects Grendel or Jenna to pop out of nowhere and usher them back to the cellar.

The room remains empty.

Mother and daughter climb out of the cellar where Stacey was convinced they would die. Her eyes adjust to the light. It's a musky, shabby little room, sparsely furnished. The stubs of several spent flares lie by the fireplace.

Stacey picks up Krista and hugs her to her chest. She tiptoes to the door. Opens it. Bright morning light shines through.

Bound by the frame of the door is a brown-grey, winter forest.

Hope beckons. Stacey plunges through the door with Krista in her arms.

Her only plan is to run as far and as fast as she can.

⊰ 5:7 ⊱

The forest passes beneath Jenna. Her thin, membranous wings propel her toward the cliff face where she left Bill.

Grendel should be done feeding by now—if the wolf left him any.

Jenna is confident things will turn out as she plans. She successfully turned humans before, but it has been many decades since the last. Jenna expects to soon enjoy a pair of very charming, *sensuous* companions.

She will allow Stacey to fret in the dark basement for hours—let the darkness and fear for her daughter render her malleable. Then, if necessary, Grendel can make an appearance to push the woman over the edge.

Jenna flies on in her true form. She is cloaked in shadow, so that an observer far below who happened to look up would simply think that a wisp of fog or cloud scudded quickly across the sky.

Smoke from a fire rises through the trees just ahead. Jenna has a moment of doubt. Her attention is diverted, and she fails to note Tyka, with Bill on her back, trotting down the trail far below.

With a few more vigorous flaps of her muscular wings, Jenna arrives at the scene of an incipient forest fire.

The mutilated but recognizable body of Grendel lies near the flames. He already smolders.

The vision betrayed me. The wolf didn't kill Bill, she killed Grendel. My poor boy!

For the first time in many generations of men, Jenna tastes fear. Things have gone terribly awry.

As she flies with top speed back to the cabin, Jenna decides to end things quickly.

I'll rend all three of them to shreds. The damned wolf, too.

Fuck it. I'll just try again. After all, the world is full of likely targets.

⚔ 5:8 ⚕

Stacey unknowingly follows in Bill's footsteps of two days previous. Krista is heavy, but Stacey, determined to go on until she collapses, trudges forward.

She doesn't get far.

Something approaches from the path ahead.

Stacey looks to the left and right—desperate for some kind of cover.

Too late. A huge dog rounds the bend in the trail. Draped across its back is the body of a man.

Stacey freezes.

It's not a dog. That's a wolf.

Tyka trots up and halts in front of Stacey and Krista. Bill rolls off her back and lays on the ground, motionless.

At first, Stacey doesn't recognize Bill. The man lying on the ground is a tattered rag doll and weighs about thirty pounds less than the Bill who kissed her on the cheek a week before in the kitchen of their home. His face is grizzled with whiskers, and the wavy hair is now more white than black.

My God. It's Bill. He looks like an empty shell.

Stacey stands there blinking in the sun. The forest is too bright, and spots swim across her vision.

Krista's sudden cry of "*DADDY!*" is the only thing that prevents Stacey from fainting. If the wolf—which appears to be terribly burned—begins to speak, Stacey will not be surprised.

She puts Krista down, and the girl throws herself on her father. Bill is still alive—but, not by much.

Stacey's attention is drawn to the wolf.

Tyka snarls at the sky.

A winged demon descends with a shriek. It's Jezebel, in all her hideous fury. The creature has huge sable wings and three inch talons at the end of muscular, hirsute legs.

Jezebel lands on Tyka and sinks her talons into the wolf's hide.

Tyka jumps and twists and tries to snap back at a flapping wing. The writhing mass tumbles off the trail and disappears into the cover of mountain laurel.

The fight makes a terrible sound that fills Stacey's consciousness, until she realizes that she is screaming as well.

The combatants roll back into the clearing of the path some yards up the trail.

Stacey sees that the wolf is getting the worst of it. The monster—bat wings flapping, teeth gnashing, claws ripping—is killing the poor beast. The cries of the wolf remind Stacey of Jeff when Grendel snapped the dog's spine.

Jezebel tears clots of fur and flesh from Tyka's back. In desperation, Tyka does a half-flip with her entire body. One membranous wing comes within reach. Tyka snaps at it and tears a gaping hole in the thin tissue.

Now, Jezebel is the one to shriek—a piercing scream that pummels human eardrums.

"YOU KILLED MY SON!" It's not the voice of a lovely coed, but the throaty cry of an enraged beast.

Razor-sharp fangs fasten on Tyka's throat and tear her flesh to the bone.

Jenna/Jezebel turns away from the dying wolf. Her body ripples and morphs from the bat-like hag into the beautiful young woman in a few seconds. A bright line of blood trickles heavily from a gash next to her left shoulder blade. More blood gushes from a bite in her throat and paints her perfect breasts scarlet.

"Stacey, I...," Jenna begins, but she doesn't get the chance to finish. She throws up her hands in an attempt to ward off the rock Stacey brings down on her skull.

Jenna staggers back. A river of blood runs down her nose from a gash in her forehead.

"Wait," Jenna says, and Stacey brings down the rock as hard as she can. Jenna's skull makes a sound like a coconut dropped on a sidewalk. She falls to her knees. Her body ripples, transforms, and becomes the hag Jezebel again.

The rock comes down again. Thick, yellow fangs shatter into fragments. Stacey raises the rock again—rears up on her tiptoes— and brings it down, double-handed, with all of her remaining strength. The hag's mottled face splatters like a too-ripe melon.

Jezebel lies twisted and mangled at Stacey's feet. One broken wing flaps intermittently—but that's it. Stacey drops the dripping rock. She faints.

Krista does not see any of this—has experienced enough to fill a thousand nightmares. Her face is buried against her father's chest.

Bill, terrified and helpless, watched the entire fight. He is filled with love and pride for Stacey.

Off to one side, Tyka lies dying. Her last vision is of a cobalt sky through bare and spiny tree branches. With her final breath, the wolf understands that she has accomplished some great good—has fulfilled her purpose.

Tyka experiences the sensation of weightlessness—and is gone.

Jezebel rises.

Bill hugs Krista tighter and waits for the end.

With not so much as a look at Bill or his family, the demon crawls off into the mountain laurel thicket.

A minute later, a terrible wail echoes through the forest. A dark shadow—at once corporeal, but increasingly blurry and amorphous—flits off through the trees.

Is that it? Is she really gone?

Bill wonders how he will find the strength to get his family out of the woods. He holds Krista tight. Stacey is just coming around.

Three men appear. They gape at the Miller family lying on the ground not far from the burnt, mutilated carcass of a wolf. One of the guys is a uniformed cop, and another holds an object Bill has longed for all week long—a sleek and shiny .357 Glock.

Epilogue

⇥ 𝕰:1 ⇤

Bill hardly remembers the walk out of the woods.

The fever returned, and he came close to death in the Braddock County hospital. In the midst of fevered dreams, he imagined that Stacey and Krista were still in Jenna's clutches—or that she was scratching at his hospital window, begging to be let in.

But, after two days, he woke to real sunshine shining through the window in a blaze of glory.

Stacey and Bill tell the police everything that happened—minus the supernatural elements. Bill explains to Jim Cook that the wolf killed Grendel. Stacey tells everyone that Jenna simply left her and Krista in the basement and never returned.

Bill gives Cook Jenna's letter and falsely admits to fleeing the hospital as per instructions from Grendel—delivered verbally to

Bill at the house before the storm hit.

Bill and Stacy's stories remain remarkably consistent. They lie when necessary. The answer that serves them best on numerous occasions is a simple, "I don't know." The questioning is tedious and repetitive, but after hours of grilling, it's finally over.

Jim Cook believes parts of the story, but like everyone involved in the investigation, he is frustrated by the dearth of captured suspects. They had no success in tracing the source of Jenna's tuition payments beyond the numbered Cayman account. Police could find no previous addresses and no record with the Department of Motor Vehicles. Cook has no way of knowing Jenna had another mode of transportation, and will not connect her lack of a car with the winged shape on the hospital security tape in his darkest dreams. Apparently, Jenna Wade simply walked out of the Black Moshannon and disappeared.

The fire started by Grendel's flare burned nearly a hundred acres of forest before a steady rain put it out. His massive body was reduced to a charred skeleton. His identity remained a mystery. The Harley was discovered in the woods near the trail head on the Calumet side of the river—the bike was stolen from a private residence near Pittsburgh the previous December.

Both Grendel and Jenna remained a blank slate.

And, what was a grey timber wolf doing in Pennsylvania?

"Fulfilling its purpose," Bill Miller would say—if anyone asked him.

Jim Cook doesn't ask Bill about the wolf, but like the other investigators, and the biologist called in from Penn State to examine the carcass, he was intensely interested in the wounds on the animal. Everyone agreed that the gouges and slashes looked as if the wolf had been attacked by another animal.

The presence of a new gasoline-powered generator deep in the woods with no path broad enough even for an ATV was a curiosity, but also a potential lead. The police traced the machine to a local *Farm Supply*. Questioning of store employees revealed that it was purchased by a man fitting Grendel's description—who'd paid in cash.

The disc left in the DVD player in the cellar solved the murder of Amy Wendell—after violating and savagely beating her, Gren had crushed the woman's skull.

Over time, Jim Cook lets it go as much as he is able.

While enjoying his retirement fishing the trout runs of southwestern Pennsylvania, Cook keeps recalling the mangled corpse of the wolf, a beautiful coed that vanished as mysteriously as she appeared, and the hospital tape with that ephemeral shadow in the shape of—well, he couldn't say.

As the years pass, and before senility quiets his creeping unease, the retired detective finds that, for him, the "realm of possibility" had become immense and borderless.

E:2

ill Miller's notion of possibility is without limits. He is a "true believer." Human doubts intrude from time to time, but the skepticism of his academic mind does not return to mitigate his belief in the incredible and miraculous.

In moments when doubt threatens to intrude, Bill remembers the timely whirlwind, the wolf gently nuzzling him as he lay near death—the rays of light shining on the river far below. Grendel was within seconds of squeezing the life from him on *three* occasions. A tornado struck his house in the precise ten second window of time that was necessary to save him; Jenna herself thwarted the monster by the river; and, *a wolf in Pennsylvania* appeared at just the right moment to kill the monster—his son.

Bill does not believe, he *knows*, that even in a universe of infinite possibilities, such things do not happen without design.

He comes to believe that he is a part of some larger plan and purpose.

His faith in God is a tremendous comfort—a lifeline for which Bill will find a desperate need.

The media coverage surrounding the twister and Billy's deliverance from death assumed sensational dimensions when the boy's father disappeared from the hospital and the story was linked to two local murders.

David and Ruth Simmons of Dunbar, West Virginia, watched the news coverage with deranged zeal.

On the very day Bill wakes in the hospital to full consciousness, Billy is snatched from the pediatric wing a floor above his head.

Bill's existence assumes a surreal quality. After his release from the hospital, he and Stacey pace the confines of a Marriott suite—provided by the Red Cross—for two days. Krista stays with Issy. Police come and go from the hotel. They ask questions to which Bill and Stacey have no answers.

Stacey spends long periods of time in the bathroom. Bill frequently pounds on the door, afraid she has done something to herself. "Leave me the fuck alone," is her typical response.

Bill stares dumbly at the television bolted to the wall for hours. A mantra cycles over and over through his mind: *This isn't real. This isn't real. This isn't real.*

After forty-eight hours, Dave and Ruth Simmons come forward and turn themselves in to the police.

Exhausted from lack of sleep, Bill and Stacey watch the pair of lunatics on the television as they are led by police into a district justice office for preliminary arraignment:

Dave and Ruth look like a kindly, middle-aged couple—all smiles and friendly waves at the cameras. Uniformed police hold back a crush of reporters swarming just outside the doors of the court. The reporters shout questions at the suspects and thrust microphones forward.

An informational banner runs across the bottom of the TV screen: *Local "Miracle Boy" Murdered.*

Dave Simmons bellows in triumph: "We serve God's grand design!" He disappears with his wife into the courtroom.

Stacey claws deep grooves in her face with sharp nails. Bill gags and sinks to his knees on the carpeted, hotel room floor.

A voice of despair Bill doesn't recognize speaks. "Fuckers didn't have the decency to tell us first," Stacey says.

The broadcast returns to the news studio. A pretty blonde anchor reports that Dave and Ruth Simmons told police they were "compelled" to act as they did. According to the couple, "God's mighty hand in delivering Billy" from the tornado was clearly discernible.

The news program turns to sports.

Bill and Stacey curl into fetal positions on opposite sides of the hotel room. A low whine escapes from Bill. Stacey hugs her knees to her chest and rocks back and forth.

For Billy's parents, every second becomes agony.

In their warped and unfathomable calculations, Dave and Ruth Simmons concluded that "God's mercy" required a sacrifice.

They drowned Billy in their bathtub.

The story goes national. A monumental but brief public outpouring of gifts and sympathy are directed to the Miller family.

In the days before the funeral, Bill's grief is prodigious. Anguish creates a vacant place inside his gut that cannot be filled this side of eternity. The mantra in his mind becomes: *Why? Why? Why?*

Stacey torments herself with thoughts of the toddler's last moments. *How terrified he must have been!* She imagines Billy's tear-streaked face, his cries turning to gurgles as he's pushed beneath the water in the tub... A part of her mind finally cracks. She compartmentalizes the broken part—tucks it away in a dark corner.

Issy handles the funeral arrangements and cares for Krista.

Bill and Stacey bury their son.

The world moves on.

In the weeks following Billy's funeral, Stacey nearly drowns herself in vodka and sleeping pills. Issy tends to Krista, holding her and rocking her to sleep.

After three weeks, Issy slaps Stacey's face twice, hard.

"You have a daughter!" she screams.

Stacey's eyes grow wide when she realizes how far she'd crawled inside her own misery. *Mom should have slapped me harder.*

Stacey taps a deep, primal strength at the core of her being—and smothers Krista in hugs and kisses.

Bill doesn't lose his faith. He believes—and curses God with bitterness and anger.

The desire to touch his son's face—or, to hear him laugh, just one more time—is so overwhelming that Bill spends much of his time weeping silently, face down on the floor.

When Bill escapes to sleep, Billy is alive and happy. *He's alive after all!* Bill cries with joy in these hyper-real dreams. Then, he wakes. The pain is like someone hit him in the middle of his chest with a sledge hammer.

The mantra cycles endlessly through Bill's mind: *Why? Why? Why?*

Unable to sleep one night, Bill drives to a park outside of town and walks to the middle of a soccer field. The night is crisp, and stars shine brightly in the early February night. Bill sinks to his knees and tilts his chin to the sky.

"WHY?" he screams.

A vision of the light on the raging torrent of the Little Kittanning River fills his mind. An answer occurs to Bill, as clear as if a voice spoke softly into his ear.

A spark of hope burns bright.

Bill comes to believe—*feels assured*—that Billy has been ushered into the presence of the "Almighty."

Not doubting his own sanity for a single moment, Bill's cries of anguish turn to tears of joy.

I believe. I REALLY believe!

tacey does not reconcile with Bill. He is changed—is not the same man with whom she'd fallen in love. Even if he had been, she finds the notion of forgiveness inconceivable. Stacey harbors some measure of hatred for him, and as irrational as she knows it to be, can't help but blame Bill for the loss of their son.

Finding the complete absence of love toward her former lover and husband of eight years a curiosity, Stacey examines this incongruity in a detached, intellectual manner. She experiences the loss of Bill from a distance, and recognizes that the place in her heart for love of him is a void she will not fill—another item compartmentalized and stowed away in the dark attic of her mind.

The estranged couple bypass the lawyers, agree to share custody of Krista, and arrange for an easy three hundred dollar divorce.

Krista will spend about sixty percent of the time with her mother, forty percent with Bill.

Krista takes the rest of the school year off. She loses weight, feels dispossessed, and walks around much of the time like one of the living dead. In the first weeks after Billy's death, Krista would simply have crawled into a fetal position to wait for death if not for Issy, who held her for hours every day.

Grendel and the events surrounding his appearance are too frightening to recall, and are mercifully repressed by Krista's psyche.

As the winter passes to spring, Krista finds that the emotional pain, which had originally filled every waking minute, becomes blunted. When the school buses stop running, she realizes that she's miserable only *half* of the time. Over the summer, Krista discovers that she can find pleasure in life again, even if it's something as simple as Sponge Bob or looking forward to school in the fall.

But, soon after Krista's sixth birthday in August, a new bomb falls—not entirely unexpected.

Even a child could not have missed Issy's failing health.

Krista is forced to absorb and negotiate truths that many adults never can: life is cruel, brutal, and unfair.

Her grandmother dies in August of the pancreatic cancer she could not beat.

Stacey and Bill work overtime to make Krista feel loved after Issy's passing. Bill assures Krista that there is love in the world, and a loving God commands ultimate good for those who choose to follow Him.

Bill believes he gets through to her. Krista is filled with hope when a spark kindles an exciting notion—the idea that she will see Grammy Issy and Billy again in circumstances more happy than she can imagine.

Krista knew about "Heaven" before—had picked it up some-where—but her father makes it seem more than just some invisible place in the sky. His eyes are so steady and confident as he talks of God's wonderful plan for them.

Bill also has a strong desire to share his faith—and the comfort it brings—with his ex-wife. He still loves Stacey, and the thought that she should suffer needlessly torments him.

When Bill raises the idea of prayer, Stacey becomes angry.

"Just what kind of all-powerful God sanctions the existence of creatures like Jenna and Grendel, Bill? Where was your fucking god when those lunatics drowned our son?"

Bill has an answer, but the anger in Stacey's eyes is so frightful he decides to revisit the topic later—much later.

Stacey resolves that she will not fill Krista's mind with false hope and "fairytales."

I'll shower her with a mother's love—but I'll also make her tough.

The diminished family comes to recognize that life does indeed go on. Bill and Stacey deal with the unwelcome knowledge that demons and monsters are "for real" in their separate ways.

Bill uses his god as his shield against the Jennas and Grendels of the world and his own inner demons.

Stacey converts negative emotions and the threat of despair into vigor and drive. She returns to the office as a paralegal and enrolls in the Saturday and evening law program at Duquesne University.

In three years, she passes the bar exam.

Stacey's career, and her devotion to Krista, is remarkable. Having been face to face with evil incarnate, Stacey sublimates the horror of her experience with Jenna and Grendel and channels that negative energy into positive outcomes. Krista is the centerpiece of her life. A typical day for Stacey involves ten hours at the office, helping Krista with her homework, and staying up late into the night to work on cases.

But, it is also true that a tiny chink in the armor of Stacey's sanity appears as a consequence of her brush with diabolism. Faculty and students in class, and later, seasoned lawyers at the office, note a strangeness that sets Stacey apart. A look in her eyes warns folks that they'd better not attempt any unfairness. Even the self-righteous and privileged old ladies in the grocery store dare not block an aisle when Stacey rounds the bend.

Sometimes, unbidden thoughts of Grendel and Jenna intrude. In a perverse way, Stacey almost welcomes these moments.

"Let them come!" she says to the dark surrounding her solitary bed. Fists clenched, she smiles in bitter triumph as she recalls the sound the thing's skull made when the rock cracked it.

Stacey rarely allows her thoughts to dwell on notions like Jenna's antediluvian origins, or the nature of the thing's progenitor.

And, only once is she brave enough to consider what her choice might have been if she did not spot the handcuff key on the cellar floor just before the light went out.

ꙮ 𝔈:4 ꙮ

𝔅 ill does not get tenure at Glenville State. His dossier is adequate, but not a slam dunk; and, while he'd properly disclosed his relationship with Jenna, the events that brought so much notoriety to the campus are held against him. No matter. Promotion to associate professor and job security, practical considerations to be sure, are trivial concerns. Bill has seen the "Glory"—been face to face with the "Devil"—and so, campus politics and career advancement are not so very scary!

He rents a two bedroom townhouse and makes a living with fixed term appointments at the Braddock County Community College, supplemented by various adjunct positions. The central elements of his life are the pursuit of his own spiritual development and fostering the same in his daughter.

Bill misses Stacey—is deeply saddened at yet another loss—but is grateful when she finds a way to pull herself up. He still loves her, and always will.

But, when Stacey remarries three years after the hell they had gone through, it's like losing her all over again. Not for the first or last time, Bill wallows in self-pity. He drinks to excess for several months, frequently cancels his classes, and questions God's purpose in making him suffer.

As it turns out, Jerry Sadler is a very nice man. With a twinge of jealousy, Bill observes that Krista adores him. And, Stacey occasionally looks like she just might be happy.

Over time, self-pity turns into gratitude. Bill looks past his self-interest and sees that things are turning out remarkably well.

With awe, Bill believes he's beginning to discern the unfolding of a cosmic plan beyond his mortal comprehension.

Krista is happy much of the time—to all outward appearances, a remarkably well-adjusted child. She is very quiet in school but gets all A's without breaking a sweat. The night terrors do not return.

By the time she turns nine, Krista comes to love her mother's new husband. She realizes that she is quite lucky—or, the way her Daddy puts it—blessed. Krista has *two* fathers to love!

She doesn't remember anything about Grendel or the events in the cabin. A shadow stains her mind, nonetheless—a seldom felt but lingering sense of something not quite right with the world.

When her mother joins the firm where she had worked as a paralegal for so many years, there is a big party. Everyone gets along, and it does not feel at all unnatural to anyone when Bill kisses Stacey on the cheek in congratulations. Stacey has not forgiven Bill, but she no longer hates him. Miraculously, some wounds have healed.

The Miller family knows that scars last forever. However, for eleven year old Krista, the night of the party brings the return of something close to unblemished happiness.

ill does not remarry, nor does he date. Since recovering in the hospital after the nightmare in the woods, he has no sexual desire. It is not a physiological problem. He observes attractive women with admiration and enjoys talking to them—but feels no need or desire for anything more.

Now and again, an attractive coed makes a pass (Bill's good looks returned with his health), but he gently rebuffs them. Bill sins daily in any number of ways, but lust is not among his faults. He has been purged of sexual desire, and whether it's a by-product of having been drained by Jenna—or something else—Bill welcomes it as a gift.

What better way to facilitate spiritual growth than to be released from the bonds of the flesh?

Bill attends services at different churches and tries a variety of denominations, but he finds no home. Not looking for spiritual nourishment, his occasional attendance is for the purpose of strengthening those in the congregation who need it. To his surprise, he finds that this genuine Christian attitude is resented almost everywhere he goes.

Bill's spiritual gift—aside from his faith—is discernment. Looking at the faces in the churches he visits, he sees a lot of people hedging their bets, doing things for show, and attending services for the social and entertainment value. Bill is not disappointed or discouraged, but he decides to worship at home.

As years pass and Krista grows, he introduces the tenets of his faith to her in a more substantial way—not pushing, but tending the slender shoot of faith that sprouted from the planted seed.

Stacey is diagnosed with pancreatic cancer at the age of forty-four. In the last weeks, her suffering becomes immense. Powerful narcotics only partially blunt pain that breeds desire for death. Bill is there for her, but retreats when he sees that she naturally prefers the comfort of her husband.

Fourteen-year-old Krista is not informed until the ugly truth can no longer be concealed. She retreats and regresses at times to become like a petulant seven year old—feral and withdrawn. Her mother's rapid weight loss and thinning hair force a reality upon her that she is unwilling to accept. She listens to music alone in her room, or else hangs out at the mall with friends in a desperate pretense of normalcy. Krista simply is not there for her mom in the last weeks. She will always regret it.

Bill sees Stacey for the last time as she lies near death in the hospital. Her cheeks are sunken. Lines of pain wrinkle her forehead. Her scalp is clearly visible through grey hair denuded by chemotherapy.

Bill wants to put on a brave face, but breaks into sobs at the sight of the only woman he will ever love. He kisses Stacey's hand and sprinkles it with warm tears. "I'll never stop loving you."

Stacey does not respond. Her eyes are open, but the closeness of death and the pain medication has robbed her of lucidity. She has no final words for Bill.

He leaves her in the hands of his god.

Two days later, Bill gets a call from Stacey's husband informing him that she has passed.

Stacey's last thought: *I should have made Krista tougher.*

She is buried beneath the earth four months after the initial diagnosis.

After Stacey's death, alone and unable to pray, Bill thinks: *Life is cruel and unfair. No amount of faith or spirituality can begin to fathom the great mysteries, or discover God's purpose in the suffering of those creatures he purports to love. Every day people die in extreme agony. Some emit anguished screams with their final breath—betrayed and consumed by their own bodies.*

⊰ E:6 ⊱

Krista comes to live with Bill full-time. The Miller family
has been effectively halved.

For a time, life in the townhouse is empty and unreal.
To Bill and Krista, their existence does not feel as if it is the same
lifetime where a family of four with a dog named Jeff once shared
a comfortable and loving home.

The look of her mother, eaten from the inside by her own
treasonous body, haunts Krista. She soon becomes unmanageable.
Her grades drop precipitously, and she is suspended from school
repeatedly for abusive language and disruptive behavior. After her
father goes to sleep, she sneaks out of the townhouse to drink and
smoke weed with her friends.

Krista and Bill grow apart with alarming rapidity. She comes
home from school and darts directly for her bedroom. At meals,
she avoids eye contact with her father. Bill tries to talk to her, but
his attempts become feeble and strained. Eventually, "How was
school?" and "Okay," become the sum total of their conversations.

With a subtle and subconscious shift, Bill's prayers morph from,

"What do you want me to do, God?" to, "Why is this happening to me?"

Shortly after her sixteenth birthday, Krista runs away from home.

Bill does not see or hear from his daughter again for three years.

After Krista runs away, Bill becomes frantic. He pesters the police daily, but they soon lose interest in the common occurrence of a teenage runaway. Bill takes a leave of absence from work for a semester and does nothing except think about and search for Krista. He spends weeks driving around Glenville—and Pittsburgh—hoping to get lucky and catch sight of her on the street. Almost three years after Krista leaves, Bill still cruises the streets some nights early into the morning—unable to let go of hope.

Throughout Krista's absence, Bill fails to think and carry himself as he knows a Christian should. He curses God and questions His purpose with bitterness and anger. But, Bill turns back to his faith over and over—unable to let go of the only lifeline he knows.

With his entire family gone, a strange notion occurs to Bill as he lies awake in bed one night: In some mysterious and unfathomable way, things are working out as they should. The idea seems ludicrous, and he wonders whether he has lost his mind.

But, somehow, Bill *believes it*.

One day, Krista shows up at the door with an infant in her arms.

Bill's daughter has grown into a beautiful young woman, but he can see lines of care in her face. She has the look of many Appalachian women he's seen in southwestern Pennsylvania and West Virginia—attractive in a down-to-earth way, but world-weary, even at a tender age.

Krista does not speak of her whereabouts, or what she has done. Bill doesn't press her.

The baby is a noisy, smelly, little treasure.

"What's his name, sweetheart?"

"I named him after his granddad and his uncle," Krista replies. "His name is Will."

Bill embraces Krista for a long time—afraid to let go. Then, he holds his grandson for the first time.

Krista stays with Bill for a week. She sleeps a lot, and her father watches her sometimes as she breathes softly and evenly in her old room. At times like these, it seems like the cares on her face melt away, and he's looking at his baby girl untouched by the world.

Sitting in the living room one evening, Bill marvels to see his child holding Will, rocking his grandson to sleep. There is little talk.

When he kisses his daughter and the baby goodnight, Bill sees a desperate longing in Krista's eyes.

Somehow, he knows she will not be staying.

Bill cups Krista's chin in his hand with a father's gentleness, and drinks in her beautiful eyes—so much like her mother's.

He points at the ceiling—skyward. "Don't forget what I told you." Then, he smiles, gives Krista a wink, and goes to bed.

She's gone the next morning. There's a note on the refrigerator. It reads simply: "I'm sorry, Dad. Take care of Will for me. Love, Krista."

Three months later, a cop knocks on the door to ask Bill to identify Krista's body. They found her slumped in a chair inside a filthy Wheeling, West Virginia movie theater—a victim of alcohol poisoning.

When Bill looks at her face on the mortician's gurney, she doesn't look like his little girl, or the grown-up mother she became. She's just a lifeless statute—beaten down and weathered by the world.

When Bill kisses Krista's forehead, it feels like cold marble.

⚜ 𝔈:7 ⚜

When Krista dies, grief gnaws at Bill's vitals for a long time. After a while, it feels like there is nothing left inside.

In time, grief turns to poignant nostalgia.

He took a picture of Krista and the baby before she left. It will grace the fridge for the remainder of Bill's years. In the photo, Bill sees the "Glory" shining through the world-weary sadness of Krista's eyes.

Bill no longer asks, "Why?" Instead, he prays, "Tell me what to do."

He accepts that the answers will come—eventually.

Bill has found his mission—sees his purpose clearly.

Raising his grandson is his mission, and Bill is filled with joy at the privilege.

Repentance is required for the various sins he still commits, but as the years pass, it comes easier and easier—and becomes a necessity far less often.

Having lost his entire family, fear of loss does not haunt Bill. He will plant the seed, keep a watchful eye, and love the boy.

Bill blinks, and diapers and regurgitated baby formula are things of the past. He blinks again, and Will is older than his Big Billy had been when he was taken.

Blink.

Bill puts Will on the bus for his first morning of kindergarten. He thinks of Krista and does not bother to wipe the tears from his cheeks.

Will returns Bill's love—as sharp as his mother.

The little guy calls him "Pappy."

⚜ 𝕰:8 ⚜

Bill marvels at the man he has become.

One morning, he looks in the mirror and has no trouble imagining the old man in his future.

And, I'm loving every minute of it.

His joy is in Will.

At fifty-one, the single defining component of Bill's life is this: He is a single, full-time grandfather of a five year old boy.

Bill objectively sees greatness in the boy, and for the most part, merely steps aside to watch that greatness grow and flower.

Years pass like the rapidly flipped pages of a book.

For some time, Bill helps his grandson with his homework in the evening. Soon, Will explains his studies to Bill.

By thirteen, Will leaves his public school classmates (and teach ers) far behind. He is interested in everything and likes to learn for the sake of learning.

A few friends come and go, but Will is too far advanced to relate to kids his own age. Bill notes that the boy is sensitive, polite, and well-mannered, especially with his elders.

They never find a church they're comfortable with, but Bill observes with approval that Will seems to take Christian principles to heart—and applies them.

Occasionally, Bill reflects on his now distant brush with that which is monstrous.

In the early years after the demons wrecked his life, he had dreams where a winged Jenna, beautiful and alluring, would appear outside his bedroom window. He would open the window, and she'd swoop in with all her hideous fury. On the mornings after those dreams, he would feel physically drained and weak. Eventually, the dreams faded and ceased altogether.

After the dreams, only two events Bill thinks of as supernatural intrude upon his later years—one pleasant, the other far less so.

Only a week after the cop knocked on the door heralding the news of Krista's death, she appeared in Bill's townhouse. He woke in the middle of the night to see Krista standing by Will's crib. He could see the bars of the crib and the sleeping child through Krista's midsection.

She stood there for at least five minutes without moving—simply looking at her son. Bill was mesmerized, and did not dare speak to his daughter. In some way, he felt that would have been ungrateful.

After a while, Krista simply vanished through the wall.

The second episode reminds Bill that though God may be in control, in the present dispensation, other unsavory entities roam the world.

Driving down the road with Will, Bill sees it hanging upside down from a telephone wire—some sort of creature, bat-like but humanoid with dun wings folded around its hirsute body.

It isn't Jenna—but, of the same order.

Bill observes with horror that he's able to discern the thing's nature, which is both lurid and lascivious in the bright noon sunshine. The wire droops low from the heavy burden.

Will spots it too, but when Bill slows to get a better look, the thing alights with a great flap of its wings.

This is in downtown Glenville, yet no one else sees it. A woman putting a quarter in the meter looks up when the great wings make a whirring sound, but she witnesses nothing but the rebounding wire.

Later, Bill explains to Will that things like the creature they saw pose a threat only to those who make themselves vulnerable by embracing depravity.

Bill does not tell Will about Steve, who, while lacking in faith, was not depraved. When he recalls the kindness of his friend, Bill can't imagine how his murder might have contributed to any "Divine plan."

Reminders like the creature on the wire tell Bill that Jenna has probably not perished, and may still be preying on others. But, he does not doubt that his part in battling her is done.

Jenna does not return to tempt Bill in his elder years. With satisfaction, and some pride—he is, after all, still quite human—Bill guesses that she knows it would be a waste of time.

⚜ E:9 ⚜

Strange as it may sound, Bill feels something like contentment with the way his life has turned out. He misses Stacey, and Krista, and Billy, and remembers them in prayer always. The pain from losing them never goes away entirely, but Bill comes to accept this as a product of his purpose.

Bill is comforted by the idea that the events of his life—even his infidelity and the loss of his family—were all, in some way, *absolutely necessary*.

While all of this is beyond his comprehension, Bill feels that, on any given day, he's exactly where he's supposed to be—that some larger plan for good is steadily unfolding.

Gradually, ever since Will came, that old feeling has been growing in Bill. It's a sense of well-being that nothing can mar.

He experienced it for isolated moments in the past: Driving over to his friend Steve's house just before that now distant horror began; kneeling at Big Billy's bedside in the hospital; falling like a dead man on a rock overlook in the Black Moshannon Forest.

But now, the feeling has evolved into something transcendent: it's more like a near-tangible *presence* that precludes loneliness.

As old age overtakes him, the "Presence" is something Bill feels upon waking, and then continuously throughout the day until sleep returns. It's like being wrapped up in a warm cocoon—or, the arms of a loving parent.

It is a feeling of joy that he can't begin to explain to his colleagues or friends. The closest word that describes it is peace.

Or, perhaps more fundamentally: Rest.

One night, not long into his sixty-fifth year, Bill lies in bed and listens to Will in the adjacent home office as he speaks for the benefit of voice-activated software. The boy's voice is deep and mellifluous. Bill cannot make out the words, but the sound brings comfort.

Will is seventeen, and will be going off to Cornell a year early.

As he listens to his grandson speak, Bill feels a sharp pain in his chest that radiates down his arm. It is a large and mortal pain that soon subsides. His breath grows shallow, but he does not desire to call Will.

He'll be sad, but I don't have to worry about that young man. His path is clear.

Slowly, that old feeling comes over Bill, more strongly now than ever before. It's as if he's wrapped up in the arms of a loved one. The feeling is not emotion, but presence—a sense of weightlessness inside a womb.

The last thing Bill experiences is the sound of Will in the other room, speaking low and confident—probably publishing some new thoughts directly to the Internet.

Bill thinks of Billy and Krista, and looks forward confidently to his reunion with them.

He whispers, "Stacey"—and feels the "Glory."

Thirteen years later, Bill's ashes long since dispersed in the foaming waters of the Little Kittanning River, Will publishes his first non-fiction book. It sells over 150,000 copies.

Over the next ten years, he writes five more that become international bestsellers.

The message of the books, while expounding on a very old and familiar theme, is presented in a novel and compelling fashion—and is precisely what a radically changed world needs to hear.

Millions of people, having read Will's books, are filled with a sense of hope and well-being, and thereafter apply principles of self-sacrifice and charity toward the people with whom they interact.

About the Author

Boris Black made a living in the halls of academe, but burned out at a relatively young age. The insipid realm of higher education was far too bleak, and so Black retreated, withdrew, and became a recluse. Now Black lives alone, deep in the woods of Pennsylvania's Laurel Highlands, where he contemplates the nether reaches of human misery and depravity. Quickly running out the clock on the latter part of his existence in this plane, the ex-professor writes dark and twisted stories for self-amusement and to lend flavor to the night sounds of the forest about his isolated cabin. Sometimes, during violent storms, or in the quiet desolation of the night, he thinks he hears voices on the heights or in the depths of steep-sided ravines.

For more, visit: BorisBlackAuthor.com.
Contact Boris at BorisBlack665@yahoo.com.